A Year in Ink

SAN DIEGO WRITERS, INK
ANTHOLOGY
VOLUME 3

Edited by Roger Aplon and Jennifer Silva Redmond

San Diego, California

A Year in Ink is a publication of
Ink Spot Press
San Diego Writers, Ink
PO Box 34374
San Diego, CA 92163

Collection ©2010, San Diego Writers, Ink
Copyright for individual works belongs to the authors.

All rights reserved. No part of this book may be reproduced or transmitted in any form without written permission from the publisher.

Editorial Committee:	Victoria Melekian, Judy Reeves, Kimberly Schultz, Nicole Vollrath
Cover photograph:	Turtle Reflection ©2004 Steve Gould
Design and typography:	Armadillo Creative

ISBN 978-0-9799204-3-1

Printed in the United States of America
Printed by Lightning Source Inc.

Contents

Introduction . . . . Roger Aplon 1

Introduction . . . . Jennifer Silva Redmond 3

Pen-y-groes . . . . Cat Saint Martin 5

Facts About Aunt Eileen . . . . Tria Andrews 6

Woman of Witness . . . . Marianne S. Johnson 7

The Dance Card . . . . John Mullen 8

The Beggar . . . . Fred Longworth 17

The Day a Box Learned Me About How
Beautiful is So Good by Wallace J. . . . . Randy Herman 18

Sabbath Fe Minus . . . . David Tomas Martinez 20

King of Sandra Day O'Connor Middle School . . . Scott Barbour 22

The Numbers . . . . Deborah Harding-Allbritain . 24

Rupture . . . . Patrick McMahon 25

Seconds . . . . Crystal Hadidian 34

7 minutes and 49 seconds . . . . Alysia Everett 36

Mindful Soup . . . . Sylvia Levinson 38

What the Dog Ate . . . . Jackie Bouchard 39

Tight Pants . . . . Jeanine Webb 42

Sandwiches . . . . Charlie Daly 44

human seeking meaning . . . . Jennifer Brooke Williamson 45

Lincoln Logs . . . . Bill Peters 46

The Persistence of Memory . . . . Oriana 48

Once Upon a Time on Thursday . . . . Amy Wolf 49

this fear of falling . . . . Lauren Wilensky 58

Fighting for Light . . . . Tori Malcangio 59

Letter Found in a Cave	Seretta Martin	61
Mother and Son	Al Zolynas	62
A Mix-Up	Jess Jollett	64
A Snail Kingdom	Eber Lambert	65
Musings of the Tin Man	Clifton King	67
Veracity	William Cass	68
47 Book Titles from My-Shelf	Gerald Vanderpot	80
Dirty Laundry	Celeste Carpenter	81
Bufo	Steve Kowit	82
The Fracture	Judy Goldstein Botello	83
The Wreck	Una Nichols Hynum	87
Changing a Light Bulb	Rick Seidenwurm	88
I Had Tea with Mary Oliver	Trish Dugger	90
The Woman Who Slept Upside Down	Sandra Block	91
all I want is to stop wanting	Lizz Huerta	96
Midwest	Jess Jollett	97
Contributors		99
Editors		107

Introduction

Before beginning the task of selecting poems for the 2010 San Diego Writers, Ink Anthology I decided on some rules: **Rule #1:** When reading unsolicited work for an anthology never set unconditional criteria for acceptances. **Rule #2:** Prepare to be surprised. **Rule #3:** Allow for humor. **Rule #4:** Put personal prejudices aside. If unsuccessful, so be it.

In making my selections I've tried to follow these guidelines and hope I've adhered to most of them. It's always tricky, this selection process. If you had a bad night or received a rejection slip in the mail, if you're fighting off the flu or have had a fight with your partner or don't have a partner and wish you had, well, all or any of these situations can jam your judgment and skew your senses. To counteract any and all of the above, I read the two hundred-fifty-plus poems submitted while sitting quietly many mornings in the sun 7000 feet above the sea in Taos, New Mexico and sipping a delightful green tea laced with mint and wild honey.

We know quite well every editor has his or her own "taste" and "vision." These natural limitations are expected to influence the selection each would make when compiling an anthology. In the publishing business it's known as an editorial signature.

So, for the record, I admit to a bias. But, that said, and respectful of my "rules of engagement," as best I could, I set aside absolutes. My hope being, the poems selected reflected the best of the work submitted, allowing for a variety of voices, themes and hues—to balance the dramatic with the comic, the traditional with the experimental, the personal with the political.

There is much to relish here. I hope the readers will find their way to the chilling as well as the sublime. These contrasting voices are much of what makes the writing community of San Diego so engaging and, I might add, unique.

My thanks to the editorial committee of SDW, Ink for inviting me to select the poetry for this year's anthology. It was an honor and a privilege.

Roger Aplon
October 2009

Introduction

When I was asked to edit this collection of prose pieces, my first thought (after "when will I ever find the time?") was, "Will there be enough good stories for another book?" I thought that the last two anthologies from San Diego Writers, Ink might have skimmed all the cream from our jug. Turns out, I needn't have worried. The cream is overflowing.

Even after ten years of reading prose by some of San Diego's finest writers, I was surprised by the level of both writing skill and storytelling talent evident in the majority of the submissions. At first picking one piece at a time to sample, before and after work, I was soon greedily devouring them by the dozens—thrilled to find myself consistently amused, intrigued, and moved.

That led to the hardest part of the job: what to leave out. Some stories I knew I would choose upon first reading them: "Veracity," "The Dance Card," and "The Fracture." With an abundance of good work to choose from, I decided to limit each contributor to one piece, to be able to include yet another writer's work.

However, one writer is featured twice: two flash fiction pieces, "Midwest" and "A Mix-Up," each only a paragraph long. You'll see why when you read them. It turned out that I chose a great deal of flash fiction—not because I tried to, but because so many of these spare pieces were vivid and affecting.

I enjoyed the novel excerpts, and look forward to reading many of them in their final form, but I ended up picking just one, by Jackie Bouchard, from her novel, *What the Dog Ate*, because it is a self-contained story with its own clear arc and satisfying resolution. Plus it rang true and was very funny.

Yes, there is humor to be found in these pages—some stories are darkly comic, like "The King of Sandra Day O'Connor Middle School," and "The Day a Box Learned Me About How Beautiful is So Good by Wallace J.;" some are sardonic, like "Sandwiches" and "A Snail Kingdom;" and some have a sweetly gentle wit, like "Lincoln Logs" and "The Woman Who Slept Upside Down."

This is probably because many of us subscribe to the theory that in trying times one must laugh to keep from crying. Hard times are always an odd kind of mixed blessing for literature and the arts. When humans are most challenged, we are most inspired, but in lean years, most artists are also least supported.

Luckily this hasn't been true of San Diego Writers, Ink, which, though it has struggled like any self-respecting nonprofit arts organization, has found significant support in this community and beyond. The members are all supporters, and many volunteer as well. They, like the larger community of artists here, have a strength and dedication we can all be proud of. And many of them are fine writers, as you'll soon see.

Writing, like any art form, may often stimulate us to think, or re-think, our opinions and positions, but more importantly, it should actually provoke feeling, make us giggle or weep, even laugh through our tears. That's the true vocation of art; that's its job. Your job is to open yourself to art: to read, and view, and listen; and allow yourself to react: to appreciate or be repelled, to love, hate, or pity.

And, as so many readers are also writers, hopefully many of you reading this will be inspired by these works to express yourself, in whatever way, shape, or form you are inclined. For we are only whole, as artists, when we, in the words of Langston Hughes, find time to both "Dig and be dug in return."

Lastly, I'd like to thank San Diego Writers, Ink for this opportunity and honor—I am thrilled to be in the company of previous anthology editors Thomas Larson and Arthur Salm—and special thanks to the team, especially the copyeditors, who helped all of us look our best. That's all the prelude. Read on.

Jennifer Silva Redmond
October, 2009

PEN-Y-GROES

Cat Saint Martin

I wanted to get pregnant in Pen-y-groes
in that old Welsh wood bed,
a thick-mattressed twisted-poster
with carved headboard faces who'd blessed
past family—I wanted you to sink
into me that miracle of wedding tradition,
a solstice feast waxed to quickening,
I only wanted to follow.

Instead, we were arguing,
you downstairs watching the BBC,
and me sitting in the window
next to the bed, my nightgown rain-drenched,
my psyche outside, a wild horse
running crazy in the storm.

Facts about Aunt Eileen

Tria Andrews

I don't know what they mean about Aunt Eileen when they say she is the black sheep of the family. But I know somehow this has to do with her divorce and that she has no children and that she never lasted her last semester of college. Maybe this has to do with the fact that she tells the best bedtime stories, like the one about auntie spider bringing back the sun in her web, after raccoon and rabbit and crow and all the rest had failed. Maybe this has to do with the fact that she came in costume as a mime to my birthday party and scared all of my friends, but not me. Maybe this has to do with the time she told us the true story of Thanksgiving and not the stories my mother reads to us. In Aunt Eileen's story, the white men came and took all the Indians' land, raped the women, and gave the Indians a few shell necklaces and I say what is rape and my mother throws up her hands and says, Goddamn it Eil, which is her nickname for Aunt Eileen she made up when they were kids and all six of them were quarantined in the same room with chickenpox. Maybe this has to do with her long hair and how all my other aunts (it's a secret, but Aunt Eileen calls them the Stepford wives) talk about hacking it off while she sleeps because long hair is inappropriate on a woman after forty. But Aunt Eileen is a witch, a shaman, which is a good witch and not a bad one, and everyone knows witches should have long hair and warts. Aunt Eileen does not have any warts, but she does have a mole. Maybe they mean that when her friend, David, was dying of cancer, Aunt Eileen nursed him until he could die and he had Christmas with us that year. Maybe this has to do with the fact that she lives in an apartment across the hall from Grandma now that Grandpa has died and Grandma calls her Eileen Nightingale. Maybe someday I'd also like to be the black sheep of the family.

Woman of Witness

Marianne S. Johnson

I summered in Newport as a child
in Grampa's house on Pell Street
with my cousins and Aunt Pauline
who had my mother's accent only stronger

and willful, especially when she said words
like "tampon" and "sexual relations"
in mixed company—I knew nothing,
but loved to feel the explosions, the shudders

in my mother's eyes as Pauline uttered
those tiny bombs, dropping from her mouth,
a mushroom cloud of shock and awe.
In the white-hot living room of Nanna's slip covers,

the sulfur yellow kitchen, a crucifix in each
bedroom, the word "divorcee" was buried deep
in secret earth like an unexploded shell,
carefully avoided. Even a child knew better

than to ask about absent husbands or fathers.
Single working mom when it was risqué, never
the ashtray and beehive cliché, her nurse's
hands cut the air in any conversation

with a surgical precision. But silence wears
like saltwater, and starch-white faith will pick
at wounds, rip the stitches out of memories,
seek a penance in ghost places.

In the years after the war, a world away
from her New England, Aunt Pauline
duct-taped her gray pant cuffs over her boots,
stationed herself on a hill with male scientists,

linked arms against the blast, then gathered
ashen research of mice and dogs covered
in the fallout of the Nevada desert. A woman
of witness, bombs drop again from her mouth.

The Dance Card

John Mullen

I had watched Mary Louise Baker for forty-five years, ever since we were in eighth grade together. I watched her again as she walked into the dimly lit honky-tonk and sat at a table just off the dance floor. She was single now—widowed. Her husband Wiley passed away last year, and, as far as I knew, Mary Louise had spent the last eleven months throwing herself into her work. Anyway, this was the first time I'd seen her in Guthrie's in over a year. And the first time ever she came alone.

Mary Louise joined the line a couple of times while I was on stage playing. She'd filled out some since high school, though by no means would you call her plump. Watching her dance, I could see the years hadn't lessened her boundless energy—she really kicked up her heels when we played our final song. Her boots looked new with stiletto heels taller and narrower than might be prudent for line dancing, as if they'd been selected for how much height they added to her short frame.

When my band finished playing its set, I put my fiddle in its case, walked across the dance floor to the bar, and ordered my usual beer. Cindy Davis came over and leaned her back against the bar. She flashed me her come-over-to-my-place wink.

"What d'ya say, Bill?" she said.

"Not tonight, Cindy."

Without moving her head, Cindy's gaze left my face, wandered across the dance floor to the table where Mary Louise was sitting, and then returned to lock again onto my eyes. She smiled and pushed herself away from the bar.

"Let me know if you change your mind."

I felt naked. Was I that obvious? My face burned like a set of brake lights.

"Hey, Pete," Cindy called over the music as she headed toward the other end of the bar. She took the stool next to my band's guitar player, the other bachelor in our group.

For the next five minutes I pretended to watch the pointed toe of my boot push sawdust around the hardwood, but really I spied on Mary Louise as she laughed with Helen Treadwell and Zack Cummings. It felt like high school all over again. You'd think by age fifty-nine I'd have lost some of the awkward shyness that comes with being six-and-a-half feet tall. The only thing that saved me from total ostracism in high school was basketball. Well, that and music. For a wallflower, being a musician is like having a cloak of invisibility. If you're up on the stage playing music, it's not so obvious that you never dance.

When I finished the beer, I ordered a double scotch. J. Edgar poured the drink, but kept the glass in his hand as I reached for it.

"You sure about this, Bill?" he asked.

"I need a little fortifying."

"I thought you stayed away from hard liquor because it made you sick?"

"That's just a story I made up once," I said.

J. Edgar shook his shiny, pink bullet head. "It's your funeral," he said, and pushed the drink in front of me.

Two swallows later I turned around and strode to Mary Louise's table to ask her to dance. The headlining band had started their set. The loudness of the music made conversation difficult.

"Hello, Mary Louise," I said.

Like a fool I extended my hand. She saved me greater embarrassment by shaking it, though she did chuckle a bit.

"I haven't seen you for a long time," she said.

"Long time," I agreed. I avoided her eyes and watched her full lips move when she spoke. All the moisture in my mouth had fled to my armpits. My tongue was as dry as a Dust Bowl farmer's field.

Just as I opened my mouth to ask Mary Louise to dance, a fight broke out two tables over. Jacob White hit Sam Perkins square on the forehead with a beer bottle, and Sam slid beneath the table like a dying ship sinks to the ocean floor. Jacob was taking after his dad, Farley, the town's meanest drunk.

While a couple of us men pinned a squirming, blaspheming Jacob to the floor, Mary Louise tended to Sam. Mary Louise tended to most everybody in Coopersville. She came back to town after she finished her medical studies and opened her medical practice. Most of the women in town had gravitated her way. After Doc Stebbins retired, most of the men started seeing her too, though a few of us old-fashioned types drove the forty miles to Bixby to get our medical care from Matthew Hall.

Mary Louise pulled a penlight out of her backpack-sized purse and flashed the beam across Sam Perkins's eyes. When she looked my way I could tell she was worried.

"Can you drive us to Mercy Hospital?" she asked.

The night was damp and cold. Lightning flashed a few miles to the west. I was glad I had put the shell on my pickup. My bandmates and I carried Sam Perkins across the gravel parking lot and gently slid him into the bed of my truck on a blanket. Mary Louise crawled in after him, and when she gave me a nod I cranked the engine and sped to the hospital. On the way I thought about the two times in my life I got up the nerve to ask Mary Louise to dance. On both occasions a fight broke out and kept us off the dance floor. I asked God if He was trying to send me a message, and, if so, what the heck it was.

I waited in my truck in the hospital parking lot for an hour, listening to the radio and watching rain streak the windshield, softening and blurring the lights. I thought about high school. Before he'd married Mary Louise, Wiley Baker and I had been co-captains of the basketball team and best friends. Thanks to his shooting skills and my ability to block shots and rebound, Coopersville High won the league championship in our senior year.

Mary Louise and I had seen a lot of each other in high school, but only in classes. Granted, Coopersville High only had a few hundred students, but she and I had always seemed to get seated next to one another. We'd dissected frogs together in biology, made crystals in chemistry, and studied wave motion using the strings of my fiddle in physics. Mary Louise was the only girl I felt even a little bit comfortable with. She was bubbly and friendly. I was smitten, but shy. I'd have never written my name on her dance card at the prom if my younger brother Carl hadn't teased me and threatened to paint Bill + Mary Louise inside a giant red heart on the side of our barn that faced the highway. Signing my name on that card had effectively cost me my best friend. Had tonight's fight between Jacob White and Sam Perkins occurred to keep me from suffering some other loss?

God hadn't responded to any of my questions by midnight when Mary Louise dashed out of the emergency room entrance holding her purse over her head against the rain.

"Sam's got a concussion, but he's going to be okay," she said. She tossed her large purse on the seat next to me, jumped in, and yanked on the passenger-side door. It closed with a creak and a groan.

This was the first time in our lives that Mary Louise and I had ever been alone together.

"I guess I better get you home," was the only thing I could think to say. I started the engine and headed back to Coopersville.

Neither one of us spoke for several minutes. I drove more slowly, of course, because there was no medical emergency now, and because I could still feel a buzz from the double scotch. The highway was empty. Outside the cones of light made by my headlights, the world was a deep black, the only other light an occasional lightning flash in the distance which revealed the angry clouds overhead.

"Do you ever think about the old times?" Mary Louise asked.

"Not much."

I glanced her way. Her stare gave me chills. Even in the dark I could feel the intensity of her blue-gray eyes, like an X-ray machine piercing the surface to reveal what's hidden beneath.

"Since Wiley died I've been thinking a lot about my life," she said. "What it's all about, what life is for, how I might have done things differently if I'd known..." Mary Louise bit her lip and sniffed. "If I'd known Wiley was going to get cancer."

"I'm sorry about Wiley passing," I said.

Mary Louise leaned so close to me I could feel her warmth. She whispered one word in my ear, "Liar."

She glared at me now with moist, wide-open eyes. The pickup rolled over the bumps in the highway's center line, and I jerked the wheel to bring the truck back onto my side of the road.

"Jesus. I'm not lying," I said. There had been a time when I hated Wiley, but now? I didn't know how I felt about him, but now that he was dead he certainly wasn't worth hating.

"Despite what you might think, Mary Louise, I really am sorry Wiley died. I know how much he comforted you. Like when your Mom died, even then he managed to make you laugh a little. He had a gift: he could always make you laugh."

"He could make me mad, too," Mary Louise said.

"Not for long, I bet," I said.

"You have no idea."

Her voice had a pained, knife-blade edge to it that I'd never heard before. I watched the road. She rummaged in her purse for a Kleenex and blew her nose.

"Tell me this," she said. "What happened prom night? Why didn't you dance with me after signing my dance card?"

I didn't like where this was heading. After Wiley had given me his half-hearted apology, I had been dumb enough to swear never to tell Mary Louise what happened. Wiley had thought it best that Mary Louise not know, he'd said it might make her feel bad. My hands sweat on the steering wheel.

"The reason I didn't dance with you at the senior prom is that I got sick from drinking too much whiskey and puked all over my tuxedo."

I shot her a glance to see if she believed the lie. Mary Louise frowned and shook her head.

"That's the same load of bull I got from Wiley," she said. "I didn't hear the real story—that he hit you the night of the prom and broke your glasses—until years later. Ever wonder why Wiley and I had Sara and Adam, boom, boom, in our first two years back in Coopersville and then didn't have Ben until five years later? Let me tell you it didn't take five years for the damn episiotomy to heal."

"The what?"

"Never mind."

My fuzzy brain really regretted my drinking the double scotch. "Are you saying you didn't have sex with Wiley for five years because he broke my glasses?"

Mary Louise groaned.

"Forego sex for five years? I'm not crazy. I took the pill to deny him his big family. And the reason I did that had nothing to do with your glasses. I was mad that Wiley lied. I was mad that he punched you. I was mad about *why* he punched you. I was mad that…about a lot of things."

She took a deep breath and exhaled noisily.

"You haven't answered my question," she said. "Why did you sign my dance card at the prom but not dance with me? And this time, damn it, tell me the truth."

When I thought about it, I couldn't see any reason not to break my promise to Wiley and tell her what had happened. Wiley was dead and Mary Louise was already mad.

"I didn't want to come between you and Wiley," I said.

"What?" Mary Louise blurted out. "Wiley and I weren't engaged in high school. We weren't even going steady."

"That's what I said to Wiley on prom night while we were polishing off a pint of whiskey in the boys' restroom. He got mad and said he didn't want anyone else to dance with you. I told him to go to hell. That's when he slugged me. He seemed to feel bad about hitting me. He apologized and then he said that the two of you had an understanding, but that you had to keep it a secret because of your mother wanting you to go to med school."

"And you believed him?"

"I was eighteen and tipsy. He was my best friend, and he was pretty drunk. I thought he couldn't tell a lie if he was drunk. I didn't figure out that he had conned me until after he'd come back from Vietnam and your mom had died and you still hadn't gotten engaged."

The wind gusted and rocked the pickup. Mary Louise leaned forward and laid her hands on the dashboard.

"You should have decked him," she said.

"Don't be mad at Wiley."

"I'm not mad at Wiley," Mary Louise said. "Not anymore." She sat back up. "I love him still. He had to put up with a lot being married to a doctor, and he never complained. Other than being overly jealous at times, he was a good husband and he was a great father to our kids." She waited for me to glance her way before saying, "I'm not mad at Wiley now. I'm mad at you."

"Me? Why?"

"Because," she said, "you put protecting your shy self ahead of figuring out what I wanted."

"What is it you wanted?"

Mary Louise shook her head. "I can't tell you; you have to figure it out on your own."

I managed to keep from screaming by tightening my grip on the steering wheel to the point my knuckles hurt. My head hurt even worse, like my brain was bouncing around, slamming into the sides of my skull. It hurt because I couldn't figure out what Mary Louise wanted, and it hurt because I didn't understand the logic of not telling me what she wanted. Not telling me seemed not only unfair, but downright cruel. I got so mad I almost missed the turn onto Mary Louise's street.

I swung the pickup a little wide but managed to keep it out of the mud as I pulled off the highway onto East Maple. I drove to the edge of town, stopping in front of the picket fence that bordered Mary Louise's two-story house, which was surrounded on three sides by corn fields. I cut the engine and Mary Louise opened the creaky door. We could hear a baby crying inside the house.

"Sounds like you have a patient waiting for you," I said.

"I think that's Emma, my granddaughter. Can you wait until I check? It looks like my daughter's still out with my car, so if it is a patient we may need your ambulance services again." She paused, then added, "Thank you for driving Sam and me to the hospital."

Mary Louise rushed through the rain into the house. I got out of the truck and took shelter on the front porch. A lightning flash close by lit up the rows of corn that stretched to the horizon. I counted one-Mississippi, two-Mississippi, three-Mississippi, and the thunder struck, sounding like cannon fire and rattling the front windows. The baby's cry jumped from a wail to a scream.

A minute later I heard music and peered through the screen door. Mary Louise was dancing barefoot, her young granddaughter in her arms. A skinny, blonde girl of fourteen years was explaining that she had done everything she could think of to calm her baby sister, but nothing had worked.

Watching Mary Louise dance, I thought what life would have been like with her, what it would be like now: the midnight patient phone calls, her grandkids and her daughter living at home. I didn't know if I could handle living in a household with a screaming baby, a teenaged granddaughter, and Mary Louise's divorced daughter all underfoot. I was used to a quiet, solitary life. Hard to imagine being able to function the next day if I'd been woken at two a.m. I wondered how Mary Louise managed it all these years. I sighed. She was an amazing woman. Amazing and frustrating.

It didn't look like my driving services were needed. I waved a quiet goodbye, but Mary Louise apparently thought I was waving hello. When she saw me on the porch she motioned with her head for me to come in. The baby continued to holler.

"Apparently Emma's not in the mood for Norah Jones," Mary Louise said to her older granddaughter. "Let's try some classical music."

The teenager pulled a CD from a rack next to the stereo and popped it into the player. Soon the opening bars of Strauss's "Blue Danube" issued forth, and Mary Louise circled the room with her still-wailing granddaughter. Mary Louise waltzed, stroked the baby's head, and cooed softly to her. The baby held tightly to Mary Louise's thick gray braid.

Since I wasn't being asked to help out, I looked around the living room. Individual pictures of Mary Louise's children and grandchildren stood on the mantle, and framed collages of different generations of her and Wiley's families hung on the wall behind the couch. On the desk set below the front window, I noticed several pictures: graduation photos of Wiley and Mary Louise, Wiley in his Army uniform, Wiley and Mary Louise on their wedding day, and something else vaguely familiar. I had to bend down and get close to the picture because Mary Louise had dimmed the lights.

A framed newspaper photo from 1968 of the Coopersville High School basketball team sat on the right-hand side of the desk. It was the team that won the league championship. The team led by all-star forward, Wiley Baker. Oddly, you couldn't see the lower portions of the faces of most of the players, including Wiley. Only the face of the team's center could be seen fully because he was so much taller than the others, six-feet-six-inches to be exact. And the reason that none of the team's faces besides mine were visible was that a small piece of heavy paper had been wedged between the frame and the glass. Since I was only a nose-length away from the frame, I could see, even in the dim light of the living room, that the piece of paper had been ripped in half and taped back together. The paper bore six signatures, five of them Wiley's, and one of them mine. It was Mary Louise's dance card from our senior prom.

Mary Louise still held the baby and swayed gently to the waltz, though the little girl had stopped crying and appeared to be asleep. I crossed the room, ducking as I passed under the chandelier.

"May I cut in, Mary Louise?" I whispered.

She smiled. "I thought you'd never ask."

The Beggar

Fred Longworth

He asks for a dollar,
his voice coming in spurts,
like water from a faucet
when the pressure's low.
The smell of a body long
unwashed hammers my nose.

He rocks a crucifix in his hand,
and taps a foot in synchrony,
as if the ritual of talisman and heel
keeps the concrete beneath him
from buckling.

By the hard jaw and stern lips,
I can tell. To him, I'm just a fool
who refuses to hear
the drum and bugle corps from Hell,
pounding on the underside
of the sidewalk; a non-believer
who won't do what he does —
wave a cross in counter-rhythm.

When he starts to ask again,
I meet his eyes and pat my Levis.
Whatever our tales, we're all
on the way to Canterbury.
I reach inside my pocket
and pull out a dollar.

The Day a Box Learned Me About How Beautiful is So Good by Wallace J.

Randy Herman

I seen this suit walkin' like he was somebody and i sez to him, "what's yer problem?" And he sez, "what's yer problem?" And that's when I knowed somebody gotta take this somebody into his own hands.

So i aksed him if he would please step aside into my office in the alley and he said, "This is so clishay!" which i didn't know he wuz french and eether did he cuz he said, "Pardon my french but fuck you " which if he was really french i don't think he woulda said that on accounta first of all he'd have more respec for his mother's tongue and also any ladies mighta walked by at that moment, which french guys is like that.

Well, of course no one talks disrespecful to me so i aksed him to gimme all his worldly goods to which he responded with another epitaph and even though he was a foot taller than me at least, why he starts running, so naturally i desisted him of that idea to which he starts to cry, which i could care less and i tell him maybe i'll let him live if he empties his pockets.

Duz he gots a wallet? No. He gots some quarters and a tissue and a lemon, which he said his litto girl give it him and he gots so much to live for...And a litto box. A baby litto box with it's got about nineteen colors and its made outta this paper which the box he said it's called oral strawmee or pastragami or pastrami or somethin' and i got no idea how anyone could make a box like that.

Maybe it's a inch by a inch and weighed maybe a millionth of a ounce maybe cuz its made outta paper remember. Which how could anyone do that! And how it didn't get scrunched up in his pocket i got no idea but you stomp on it probly and it wouldn't care.

Course if you try that i would hurt you on accounta this box it's very good luck for sure which at first i rote very god luck and i'm not religious or nothin' but i'm not stupid neither and this box is special. You know, like special no one else can play with it special.

Now i don't got no kid and i had a dog once what run away and got squished and so i put the box next to the picture of him by the heater and i just knowed this box was gonna be like like the kid i never had, or somethin', i don't know, and if you think i'm delicate or something, i am not delicate. That would be dangerous to suggest that i am delicate.

Well, when i seen the box, i give everything else back to the guy, which he could care less since he was mewling and drooling and begging for his life so what duz he need wit a lemon and some quarters (but he couldda used that tissue fer sure).

But i told him how he changed my life for the better and even tho i was still gonna steal stuff and hurt people, which a fella gotta honor what makes his inner heart sing, i was gonna take good care of his box (i almos wrote god again. Whoa.), which i wouldn't kill him if he didn't tell nobody bout our litto adventure and i wished him good luck with his daughter ha! Ha! Since i don't know if he really gots one but by that tine i was full of liteness (which that cud be like a lite bulb or a balloon just wants to float away) and love for the hole world and jus wanted to spress myself, so i rote down this story. The end.

Sabbath Fe Minus

David Tomas Martinez

The word weekend must come from weaken, from the language of late bars
and early living rooms, originally meaning, before distortion,
to have fun.

So many of my Saturday mornings are bayers of closing the blinds and rolling over more sleep.

If not for Sunday barbeques after basketball we would surely honor the Sabbath,
me, and the brothers I ball with,
call when there are two bat swings and a baby's breath of trouble.

Our sports have oars, engines, or darts, our favorite games are ones with balls,
ones where the object is to score through an ancient triangle, box, or hole.

The Mayans put to death the winners of their games;

and though on Sunday where I ball, none of my boys have been sacrificed, I have seen plenty of fights between friends and relatives running to their cars to pull pistols.

On Sunday, on the sidelines of the gym, I dribble and talk, slap necks and pretend
to fight, and look at the rim and at its height it seems so far,
looks so large and beautiful and so familial.

Because we are a family of weekends
weakened by drinking and weed and women in cell phone pictures
with their heads truncated, but bodies, but bodies round and supple.

And we are weak in the knees when our boy

talks about Sabertooth in the back of his truck. Sabertooth, a woman
with a perfect body and a beautiful face, but with teeth, with teeth like a wildcat.

And she is a wild cat in the red boots of our dreams.

But I am quiet because I have no stories,
my boys are laughing and say *I care too much,*
that I have *grown round and supple,* and *when am I due with her baby.*

I laugh because it's funny and because it's true.
I reached into the box of my chest and found the ball of
my heart.

My homeboys will go out but I am going home
and I know, like me, eventually they will go home
and when those prodigal boyfriends return,

they will climb in bed, like me,
wrap their arms around her waist, like me,
the wings of our shoulder blades collectively

stretching and extending over bright amens.

The King of Sandra Day O'Connor Middle School

Scott Barbour

In *The Art of War*, Sun Tzu said, "All warfare is based on deception." So I merely pretend to be a pimple-faced, red-headed, role-playing seventh grader. In truth, I am biding my time until the glorious day when I will smite my enemies and assume my proper place as king of Sandra Day O'Connor Middle School.

Sun Tzu said, "In war, practice dissimulation, and you will succeed." So when Chad Spencer trips me in the hall or shoves me into my locker, I feign fear and pain. When he calls me a fag, I fake anger. When he spits on me, I act like I'm humiliated. When he urges the girls to laugh at me, I pretend we were never friends in fourth grade, that he never invited me to his house to see his collection of polished stones.

Sun Tzu said, "The highest form of generalship is to balk the enemy's plans." So I block my father's efforts at every turn. To his face, I smile and accept his commandments and punishments, while behind his back I disassemble his power tools and poison his lawn. I scuff up his dress shoes, cut moth holes in his suits, and dilute his Grecian Formula. In these ways, I slowly erode his power and reputation among his men.

Sun Tzu said, "If in training soldiers, commands are habitually enforced, the army will be well-disciplined; if not, its discipline will be bad." So I insist that my orders be followed, even though my soldiers are lazy and lack valor. At lunch, when I demand a status report, Lee smirks his junior-chess-champion smirk and says, "Dude! Ever heard of Clearasil?" Olfanski blinks behind his big plastic glasses and mocks my *World of Warcraft* achievement status. Washington flattens my Tater Tots and describes, in disgusting detail, my mother having sex with multiple four-legged partners.

They laugh now, but they won't be laughing when victory is mine and they are my slaves. Their job will be to bring me women and watch as I perform glorious acts of sex. They will weep with jealousy and die virgins.

Sun Tzu said, "Ponder and deliberate before you make a move." He said, "Let your plans be dark and impenetrable as night, and when you move, fall like a thunderbolt." So at night I sketch battle plans in my spiral notebook. My list of names is long and growing, and the methods of death are gaining in complexity and ingenuity. Medieval torture devices, which I am currently bidding for on eBay, will be implemented to great effect. Joints will be cracked. Thumbs will be screwed. Bodies will be hugged in the eternal embrace of iron maidens. Intestines will be rotisseried before the eyes of their still-living owners. Meanwhile, a series of explosions, carefully synchronized for maximum terror and gore, will mark my ascent to the throne.

On that great day, my enemies will learn the wisdom of Sun Tzu's most crucial lesson: "Do not press a desperate foe too hard."

The Numbers

Deborah Harding-Allbritain

Every Tuesday and Wednesday morning I pick up Joe from the autism class, walk him down the school hallway, his starfish little hand wriggling in mine, as he counts the numbered doors— *Ten, nine, eight* he calls as I point to a crow on the grass: *Look Joe: bird*—nothing doing, he yanks me back to the doors, *seven, six* as if he's naming playmates. Inside my office he makes a beeline for the wall calendar, touches the dates smiling. What Joe? What do you see that I can't? And I think of Daniel Tammet, autistic savant, renowned mathematician, sitting on the hard floor of his childhood London bedroom away from the loud games of the others, reading numbers in his *Mr. Men* books opened on his lap—how he could see and feel them—the 4, shy and quiet, the loud 5, the brilliant white of 1. Joe hands me his *Three Blind Mice* book, rubs the numbers on each page oblivious to my ridiculously animated voice. I slap my hand fast over 4, 5 and 6, coaxing Joe to look at me but he screams, his beloved numbers disappeared so I let the black 7, his favorite, link arms with 8 and 9, watch them spiral off the white page. At night, under the covers, Daniel counted numbers, stopping each time at 89, nearly weeping as that magical number's soft clean snow fell in his mind, rocking him in its peaceful silence.

Rupture

Patrick McMahon

The question is out.

As if seeding a lone, ominous cloud after decades of drought, it hangs in the air as Mom leaves the room. Surely she's coming back. Surely she's just gone to retrieve an answer. All I'd written in the letter was, "There's something I want to talk about when you visit." All I'd just asked was, "What can you tell me about my adoption?"

I sit upright on my couch, firm cushions approaching uncomfortable, and wait. A clock ticks. A train whistles in the distance. What could she be doing? We've managed to successfully converse for the first time about Dad's drinking, how it affected her, me, and my younger brother. I know my mother is strong, a survivor. She divorced Dad and is doing well on her own. She would do anything for her two sons. She's accepted me as a gay man. Yet I've avoided the subject of my adoption as if it's a hammer that could shatter a glass house with a tap.

She returns after a minute or two, carrying a few envelopes, and slowly sits down in the chair next to the couch. Instantly I know what they are, though I've never seen them and did not ask her to bring them. Where have they been all my thirty-two years? There is a moment of suspension and lake-bottom quiet as she takes a deep breath and extends them to me, her face both calm and apprehensive.

Savoring this moment, yet wanting to pounce like a child in a Christmas morning frenzy, I accept the small bundle while looking into her eyes, sensing that a threshold is being crossed. Without a word, I begin to sift through the packet, and soon everything in my world disappears except the emerging papers in my hands. I see letters from the State of Illinois Department of Public Welfare, a notice of a birth registration with my name on it, and three typed pages on that long, thin, waxy paper that makes a lot of noise when handled. The words *Petition to adopt* jump off the first page, but my eyes are pulled to the most official-looking document, sheathed in a baby blue, thick paper cover. In the middle is a single word, with a space between each letter, each capitalized and individually underlined: D E C R E E.

My heart is pounding as I unfold the papers to reveal five more legal-size pages. Struggling to focus clearly, I glance through them. Words and phrases begin to take shape. *Otto Kerner…Acting Judge…1958…Petitioners to adopt BABY BOY SHIELDS*. Baby Boy Shields. Is that me?

I scan to Paragraph 4: "That Richard Shields is the father and Barbara Mizer a.k.a. Barbara Shields is the mother of the said child." My God! They have names! I silently mouth *Richard* and *Barbara*. At first, they sound like names I've never heard before. Then they echo in my mind, trying to attach to something familiar, trying to become parents. Richard—Richard Burton, Richard the Lionhearted, Little Richard. Barbara—Barbra Streisand, Barbara Walters, ancient Aunt Barbara.

With a deep sigh, I flip the waxy page and read on to Paragraph 5: "That Richard Shields, the father, abandoned and deserted his said child…" Then Paragraph 6: "That Barbara Mizer a.k.a. Barbara Shields, the mother, is unable to maintain her said child, and she abandoned and surrendered her said child to the petitioners herein."

For a moment, the floor seems to drop from beneath me. Of course I've known that in order to be chosen, I had to be un-chosen. Surely every adopted child figures that out eventually. But now here it is, all official. Two people with real names deserted, surrendered, and gave me away.

With sadness stirring in my gut and the word "abandoned" sinking into my bones, I read through to the final paragraph: "IT IS THEREFORE ORDERED, ADJUDGED and DECREED that from this date, Baby Boy Shields, a minor, shall be to all legal intents and purposes the child of the petitioners, Leonard Patrick McMahon and Joan Marie McMahon, his wife…and it shall be the same as if he had been born to them in lawful wedlock. IT IS FURTHER ORDERED that the name of the said child shall be changed to Patrick James McMahon."

Staring at this last phrase, I have to remind myself that this document is referring to me, not someone else. It's me sitting here in my funky, antiquated apartment in the heart of Kansas City, Missouri, who was born in Chicago as a Shields, abandoned, and re-forged as a McMahon.

When I realize my thumb is bearing into my temple, I stop and look up. My mother appears the same as before: petite frame, dark brown eyes, jet black hair tinged with gray, a worried expression etched into the lines on her sixty-five-year-old face. I realize just how deeply I've been terrified of losing her, like asking about my adoption might be a betrayal, might result in banishment or losing everything I've ever known as family. After all, it is Joan Marie McMahon who has raised me as her own, loved me, protected me, sacrificed for me. She is who I've always seen as Mother, even though since age five, knowing of another.

But now here I sit with that other mother's name for the first time. A name that's been hidden in a drawer or file or box for thirty-two years, a name that Mom has known and I have not. I can barely take a moment before asking the next question, the second chug of an engine straining to pull a train out of a long tunnel. "So, Mom, how did it all happen?"

Braced, surely prepared, perhaps even rehearsed, she begins to tell me the story of my origins. "Well, we'd been married ten years, and there was still no baby, so we filed for adoption. It wasn't long after that Ann Einarson approached us saying she knew of a woman wanting to have a baby adopted. She asked if we were interested."

"Ann Einarson?" Our next-door neighbor?

Perhaps acknowledging my rising pitch and lifted eyebrows, Mom clears her throat. "Yes. Well, anyway, the woman was a patient of her mother's doctor. The doctor was quite reputable, well-known, had even been on TV a couple times." She pauses as I note her emphasis on "reputable."

"We weren't quite sure about doing this without an agency involved, but he told us private adoptions were really quite common. So we decided to go ahead with it. But then the woman changed her mind. She decided to keep the baby."

"Wait, so that wasn't Barbara? That wasn't me?" I suddenly feel irked by a surprise detour.

"No, but strangely enough, it was only a few months later that Ann approached us again. This same doctor had another patient wanting to find a home for a baby. Naturally, we wondered about this doctor. You know, was he part of some sort of black market or something?"

I feel my jaw drop as she continues.

"So your dad and I met with the doctor, and he assured us it was just a coincidence to have two patients wanting to find homes for their babies. We felt he was telling the truth, so we looked for an attorney. As it turned out, one of our neighbors down the street was a lawyer and agreed to handle all the legal work. Howard Parsons. I don't think you ever knew him. They moved away when you were still a baby."

My woozy head swivels slightly. As the phrases *black market*, *telling the truth*, and *changed her mind* whirl in the air, I can't help but notice my mother's casual tone, as if this is a story she's told on numerous occasions. And yet I can tell she's nervous. She's starting to say, "You know," more often.

"Anyway, he and Ann met with them a couple of times to sign some papers. I think Ann took them some things, you know, like blankets and baby clothes."

Even with these scenes swirling, the question forms, "Why did Ann go?"

"Oh, there had to be a witness. You know, someone to verify that the right people were there when it was time to adopt you."

Ann Einarson met my parents before I was born? My next-door neighbor? Who watched me grow up? I lean back with my hands behind my head, stare at Mom in disbelief, and try to resist the growing knot of agitation in my gut.

But she seems anxious to get it all out now, and anticipates my next question trying to push its way up. "Ann said your mother and father seemed very nice. That they got along well, and had classical music playing when they were there. She also said they weren't married. That when your mother got pregnant, your father had plans to move to New York. He was a musician and wanted to, you know, pursue a career there, but your mother didn't want to move away. Apparently he left and then came back to be with her when you were born, so he must have cared about her."

My heart droops for a moment. My father cared about my mother, but apparently not about me. Did I hear *New York*? He was a musician? I glance over at my music stand displaying Mozart's Clarinet Concerto. Maybe that's why the lessons began in second grade. I suddenly love the idea of my birthfather going off to New York. How exciting. How courageous. And then just as suddenly, I'm disgusted. That he would leave after getting her pregnant. With me!

Reeling, dazed, trying to associate these less-than-honorable events with my beginnings, I scramble for pen and paper. "Mom, can you slow down a little? I think I need to write some of this down." I can't seem to shake this notion that I might not get myself to ask about this again.

Like a reporter with pen poised, I go on to the next question. A big question. "So what actually happened after I was born?" This may be the closest I ever get to my birth story. The story most everyone else takes for granted, rarely thinks twice about. The story I've never heard.

She pauses, one clenched hand covered by the other, and takes a deep breath.

"Well, I was sick with the Asian flu that was going around then and wasn't able to go to the hospital. Your dad and grandma and Ann went and picked you up. This was a few days after you were born. They brought you home. Grandma carried you in and then stayed to take care of you for a couple of weeks because I could barely get out of bed." She pauses, stares off for a moment. "It was hard not to..." Her voice cracks. "I didn't get to see or hold you much. I just didn't want to take a chance on getting you sick."

When she turns back with watery eyes, I crumple a bit, unable to write, moved by her sorrow. It's been a very long time since I've seen her upset, and the sight takes me back to the boy whose world was so easily shaken by it. How can I continue?

Yet the rush of the story keeps flooding and pushing me on. I realize I've always assumed she was there and could tell me what happened. Now the missing details seem important. What happened at the hospital? How will I ever find out? Grandma is gone. Dad is distant.

Composed again, and as if she can hear my thoughts, Mom continues, "You may want to talk to Ann. I had lunch with her a while back and mentioned that you might be calling to ask about this."

"You did?" My mind is bending into new shapes. In one corner, I imagine her anticipating this from the moment she received my letter and preparing in a myriad of ways. I slowly spin out, "Well, yeah, I probably will want to talk with her."

Staring down for a moment at the blue carpet, I pause to collect myself. Mom's anticipation is both relieving and unnerving. Just how would Mom and Ann have talked about this over their recent lunch? For an instant, I imagine Mom visiting the old suburban Chicago neighborhood, virtually unchanged, most of the adults of my childhood still living there. I picture Mom chatting with Ann over salads and sandwiches in her kitchen, the same one I passed through countless times as a kid.

Would Ann have frozen? Dropped her fork? Said something like, "Oh, Joan. Really? After all this time?"

Would Mom have been nervous? Clutched her cup of coffee? Responded, "I guess it was bound to come up sometime. Maybe it's that therapist he's been seeing. He'll probably want to talk to you."

I can see Ann's perpetually youthful face in distress. I can hear her voice so firmly implanted in my brain. "Sure I'll talk to him, if it's okay with you. Should I tell him everything? I keep seeing all these reunions on Oprah and Sally. Do you think he'll look for them? Are you all right?"

And Mom, fully recovered, might say, "Oh sure, it's okay. I'll be fine. I just don't want him to get hurt."

Shaking my head, I'm back in the room and become some sort of interviewer. Questions begin to pour out. "Mom, when did Ann meet them? Where did they live? What else did they tell her?" Just the facts, ma'am. I begin to realize I've lived all my life without asking so many basic questions. How did they come to the decision to adopt? How did they feel about finding a baby by word of mouth? How did the rest of the family feel about this? As I ask a few of these questions, I can see she's uncomfortable; she rearranges herself in the chair once in a while, but answers everything as best she can. I don't want her to feel pummeled, but now that it's all out, I can't seem to stop myself.

"So you had to go to court to finalize the adoption, right?"

"Yes. That was about six months after you were born. Otto Kerner was the judge. You know, the one that was later convicted of corruption and spent some time in jail." I cringe as she takes on an air of fond memory. "I remember sitting in his huge office and holding you in my arms. Even your dad seemed in awe of him. I remember the judge leaning forward and saying, 'Now remember, this is not a toy. You must take good care of him.'"

I look out a window for a moment and suddenly want to jump into that scene. *Your honor, how could you be so blatantly patronizing? A toy?!* When I turn back to Mom to ask why he would say such a thing, her face still looks so nostalgic. So I skip to the next thought cascading down the rapids. "Tell me about those first few months. Was I easy, or did I cry a lot?"

Mom sits back, relaxes a bit, and seems to enjoy sharing how thrilled they were to finally have a baby, how she read Dr. Spock's books, how I was an easy child, especially compared to my little brother, adopted five years later. With warmth and pride, she tells me, "I used to put your crib by the living room picture window." I'm grateful to know this, to feel loved and cared for, even as that scene begins to feel like being on exhibition.

And just as suddenly as the whirlwind began, it subsides. A lull ensues. I sit back, stretch out my legs, and stare at the bookcase across the room that houses hundreds of my albums and books. I feel like I need to touch all of them and study each one to see if it still feels like me.

I look at my mother, now drained of the tale she has held all these years. She looks tired. And yet there's so much more. And part of me wants to hear everything she's said over and over, like a new bedtime story. But I know we're done for now.

"Well, Mom, this is a lot. It's going to take some time to think about all this." Then I feel compelled to say, "But I am glad you brought it all. I'm glad you told me everything." As I sit up, I wonder if she's glad.

She smiles slightly. "Yes. Well, I guess you have a right to know." Then she sighs. I can't tell if it's from relief or worry. "I think it's time I go to bed."

"Yeah, it's getting late." We stand, both trying to find a way to simply say good night. I lean over a little and give her a hug. "I guess I just wasn't ready to ask until now." How can I explain all the recent delving into the undeniable void inside?

She holds on tight, then pulls away and gives me another small smile.

Neither of us is finding words for our feelings. Neither of us has much experience at it with each other.

As Mom retires to the bedroom, I stand and watch her walk away, then sit back down on the couch, not anywhere near ready to throw sheets on the air mattress and attempt sleep. Feeling raw and numb, I glance at all the opened envelopes resting on the end table as a hive of thoughts and feelings begins to buzz. So relieved she didn't freak out. Amazed she brought the documents with her. Worried about her being okay.

The magical, glowing decree stands out. I pick it up, rub my thumbs back and forth over its cover, slowly unfold, and begin to read through it again. Something deep in my gut stirs. I have the beginnings of my beginnings, and I'm so excited I could dance, so sad I could curl up and weep, so confused I could pace all night long. But I continue to sit.

Barbara Mizer and Richard Shields. Just knowing their names makes me feel a little more like everyone else. And it makes me think about how long I have not known, what I might have lost. I may have brothers and sisters. And grandparents.

And aunts and uncles and cousins. Do I want to find them? Would they want to know me?

As I make the bed, turn out the lights, and stretch out, the notion grows that my life has been a play, scripted and cast and carried out. Only I didn't know I was on stage. All my life, I've known of my adoption. All my life, I've not known that my next-door neighbor played a part in it. That she actually met my biological parents. How much more don't I know? And who else knows, besides Ann Einarson and Howard Parsons? Ours was a close-knit neighborhood. Did any conversation over martinis at holiday cookouts result in the revelation of my origins? Did the Hartleys know? The Reillys? The Mochels? What about the families of school friends? Our doctor? Our dentist? I can't recall any of them saying anything, but did they ever look at me and see a child with mysterious or questionable beginnings? Probably not. But right now, all I can think is, others knew more than I did.

As I lie and stare at various barely illuminated touchstones of the life I know now, my thoughts drift back to Ann. She saw me grow into a toddler, a young boy, a teenager. I must have been quite a curio for her. I wonder what she thought when my musical talent emerged, or when I displayed shyness or excelled in school or did silly, embarrassing things. Did she see either of my original parents in me? And what in the world did she think when Dad's drinking got bad?

With shadows reaching across the room from blinds blocking streetlights, newly formed questions keep floating up like rubber balls released from the bottom of a pool, silently sending out waves when they reach the surface. How many more are there? Where are they coming from?

As the waves eventually smooth out, I get up, tiptoe to the bathroom, and splash cool water on my face. On my way out, I poke my head into the bedroom. She stirs. Of course she's awake. I whisper, "Good night. And thanks."

I can barely see her as she softly replies, "No one will ever love you more than I do."

I feel a tear beginning to form. "I know, Mom. I know."

SECONDS

Crystal Hadidian

sixty - one seconds   guppies   in   a   bubbling
pond   s e v e n t y - t w o   s e c o n d s   or   those
large   goldfish   white and so   orange like
something   very   orange   fifty-eight seconds
   still   waters   somewhere there are   still
waters   sixty-seven   seconds fire   firefire   eighty - four
seconds   daggers daggers   daggers no   puppies
   and   kittens   ninety-six seconds   peaceful
  methodical   strokes   into   cool   blue   water
one   arm   s m o o t h   into coolwater   then
the other   yes   yes   cool water   bright   blue
like   easter eggs s e v e n t y - five seconds   thunder
earthquake tsunami somewhere someone   is meditating
    yes   zenzenzen yes   eighty-two seconds
explosion   get   this   watermelon   out
    ninety-eight   seconds jackhammer hammer hammer
concrete blast hammer demolition   eighty-three seconds
   relax   honey   yes honey   and jam andbread and
yes   not   much   longer   and an astroid burns
   through   atmosphere like   seventy- s e v e n seconds
another earthquake thighs lava hips robbery pelvis pain
made for this push murder push danger push fifty-two
seconds push push push like nothing you know push
seventy-four there's a terrorist between my legs ninety-nine
seconds prefer piranhas nibbling my limbs instead of   this
    human shoving its way out   tired   have I mentioned
sixty-eight tired have I mentioned dull thunder have I
mentioned sixty-six seconds waterfall   we are   breathe
   breathe sixty-nine waterwater   f a l l   yes come yes

burning push so tight push burning burning push fire burn
seventy–four seconds and I know he's coming burn push
focus push burn i n g focus   breathe   breathe   push
   breathe   eighty-five seconds soon he'll be in my arms
push be in my arms now pushfirebomb blow
oh   hello

7 MINUTES AND 49 SECONDS

Alysia Everett

Not sure how the conversation will begin or end, I nervously dial Mr. Carter's telephone number. It rings once, then twice. He picks up. With a thick country accent, he says hello. I quickly imagine him: white, late forties, and overweight, wearing faded denim overalls and a dirty white tee shirt. My heart pounding and my body shaking, I collect myself and say, "Hi. Is this John Wade Carter?"

He says, "Yes it is," in a way that also says "what the hell is it to you?"

I continue. "This is Alysia Walker. My maiden name is Everett. I am Wayne Everett's daughter."

There is a silence as he tries to bring the name to memory. He says my father's name a couple times

"Wayne Everett...Wayne Everett, doesn't ring a bell."

Do I have the wrong number? I try again.

"Wayne Everett Raines." My father had two last names: one given at birth, another thrown on after death.

There's a brief pause. I shoot out, "I just want to ask a couple of questions." I say this as quickly as possible in fear that he'll call me a nigger—as he had my father before killing him in cold blood—and then hang up the phone.

He lets out a remorseful sigh. "Oh, I see where you're going with this." He composes himself. "This isn't going to be an easy conversation for either of us."

Relieved that he hasn't hung up, I scan my mind for questions, questions that I have had for as long as I can remember. Nothing. Overwhelmed, I begin to cry and the only question I can muster is, "Why?"

"Well, I was on drugs and heavily loaded up on alcohol. I was young and I didn't care about living, I had no respect for myself or anybody else for that matter. I wasn't a racist then and I'm no racist now." His excuses pour out, almost as if he is reading from a teleprompter. He pauses. I say nothing. He continues. "I had a real big anger problem back then. I almost killed a couple of my own brothers and sisters for rubbing me the wrong way. I was really messed up back then." He's rambling. I sit in silence wanting and needing it to make sense. It doesn't.

I wipe my tears and clear my throat. "Do you feel as if your seven-year prison sentence for murdering my father was fair?"

"No it wasn't fair," he says. "I should have fried, but me frying for killing your father wouldn't have changed the situation. To be honest with you, my lawyers knew it was best to keep me quiet. I'm a very outspoken and honest person." His tone changes, as if he is proud of his "outspoken and honest" quality.

I'm hurting. The pain radiates throughout my body. And I'm lost. I think about hanging up, but I don't. I know this conversation is a vital part of my salvation. I change the subject because it pains me to hear him continue.

I ask my final question. "Do you have kids?"

He replies, "Yes, I have three." For a brief second, I envy his children. I think about them, wonder how they grew up, if they knew their father murdered a man.

Through my tears I tell him, "I've never even been to my father's gravesite."

"They didn't ship his body back to California?"

"No, he wasn't from California. He served in the Air Force and was stationed in California," I say. I feel as if he's trying to assemble an apology of some sort. He doesn't. He seems to know that a simple, "I'm sorry" would not suffice.

Instead he says, "That's right he was in the military. That's another reason I felt bad about what I did. I support our troops."

I've heard all I need to. I politely thank Carter for his time and proceed to end the call. Before I hang up he says, "Well if you ever need to know anything else, feel free to call again." Then in the most hesitant manner he adds, "I'm sorry."

I hang up. The phone reads seven minutes and forty-nine seconds.

Mindful Soup

Sylvia Levinson

While onions and garlic are sautéing,
and I am drawing fresh, filtered water,
a woman is walking many meters
to dip a bucket into a well
at a refugee camp in Uganda.

While slicing organic carrots and celery
carried home from the farmer's market,
a four-year-old boy and his six-year-old sister
are sorting food scraps
in a garbage heap in Managua.

In goes clean barley, scooped from the grocer's barrel,
while a man in Myanmar, a woman in Somalia,
are stirring a kettle above an open fire,
rice gleaned from their village's diminishing crop,
by cyclone or drought, by soldiers torching fields.

Into my garden for chard, spinach, basil,
green and fresh, planted by my own hands,
while the child in Sierra Leone whose
hands were severed during civil war,
now a young man, begs in the streets.

With each ingredient, I become smaller.
The pot simmers, I stir, taste, season.
A roadside bomb kills an American soldier and two
Iraqis, the streets of Tijuana splatter with blood. A woman
in Congo, left to bear her rapist's child.

What the Dog Ate
Novel Excerpt

Jackie Bouchard

Maggie tried to finalize the remaining projects during her last week at BioHealth, but she found it hard to concentrate—or care. Wednesday afternoon she claimed a migraine and left early holding a hand to her temple for effect, thinking: just two more days of this place.

She wanted to go straight home, but knew the refrigerator held nothing more than a half-eaten jar of kosher dills and some marmalade. She didn't need much. She planned to whip through the store, grab some cereal, milk, and ice cream, and then zip home to her dog and pajamas. This would be so much easier if someone would just invent Human Chow, she thought as she grabbed a cart and pushed it, with its rattling wheel, into the store.

She'd already hit the dairy section and stood in the cereal aisle analyzing all the different options. Oat Squares were on sale. The cost-per-ounce was less than her favorite granola, so she opted for two boxes. She flung them into the cart, contemplating the simplicity of a product named for its primary flavor and shape. She tried to think of other examples; pineapple rings came to mind. *What else? Orange Slices! Those sugarcoated jelly candies Dad used to buy.* She hadn't had those in forever. Her mouth watered as she imagined sinking her teeth into one, the burst of orange flavor, the crunch of the sugar crystals. Orange Slices would be the perfect snack for the ride home. She started to swing the cart back toward the candy when she glanced up and saw Dave with That Woman at the end of the aisle.

Maggie stared in horror and fascination. She flip-flopped between the urge to run in the opposite direction, or to get a good look at That Woman, the one who stole her husband. It was like watching a slasher film. She couldn't look away, even though it made her feel sick to see Dave and the easy, comfortable way he stood with That Woman, his hand resting at the small of her back. The way he used to stand with Maggie.

They were heading down the back aisle and hadn't seen her. The lighting was bad, with only every other florescent strip light on. Dave had his back to Maggie, but after so many years together she would have recognized the back/side/top of the man's head at fifty paces in any light. That Woman stood in front of Dave, next to the meat case, so Maggie could only see a sliver of her long wavy hair, jeans, and sweater.

They had stopped in front of the bacon.

Dave doesn't eat bacon.

They had shifted now. Dave still had his back to Maggie, but she could see That Woman's face. She danced a bacon package back and forth in front of Dave, as if to entice him with it. She was not at all what Maggie had envisioned in her tortured thoughts.

When she'd seen the lavender thong panties in the specimen bag at the vet's office, the fabric less substantial than the pink velvet cord Gram used to keep her reading glasses around her neck, Maggie had known That Woman was small. Impossibly petite. Maggie had pictured a slim comic-book vixen with long legs, no hips, and a flat stomach beneath zeppelin breasts. She'd also imagined thick blond hair and too much makeup. But *This* Woman was skinny—boyishly so. Her figure looked like she could act the part of a slice of bacon in a school play on agricultural products; it didn't look like she ever *ate* bacon. She didn't seem to be wearing any makeup. She wasn't plain, but she certainly was not gorgeous. Her hair was long and thick, but frizzy and a mousy brown color. She was…normal.

They laughed as That Woman flipped the package over to read to him. They huddled together as she pointed at the words. Dave appeared to read along.

He won't eat that. It has too many nitrates.

Dave took the package out of That Woman's hand and tossed it in the cart. She giggled, bumped him with her twelve-year-old boy's hip, and they moved on.

Maggie stood rooted to the spot. Her brain thought: Dave doesn't eat bacon. But her gut whispered: he's not coming back.

She drove home, barely noticing where she was going. She shoved the groceries into the fridge, still in the canvas bag, even the cereal. Her wedding band caught her eye. She fingered it with her right thumb and index finger and yanked it off. She pulled open the junk drawer and dropped the ring into an old Altoids tin that still smelled of mint and held a few paperclips. She slammed the drawer shut.

Tight Pants
(after Frank O'Hara)

Jeanine Webb

As for measure and other technical apparatus, that's just common sense: if you're going to buy a pair of pants you want them to be tight enough so everyone will want to go to bed with you.
—Frank O'Hara

Walking down 101 surrounded by eternal
boys and girls in endless LEVIS in the windows
tight like a good ride why yes, tight it's their
favorite Moonlight tans you've got to drag it
out just like schweeeeeet La Jolla the gaudy
retirees in hats Which is why I support the sea
lion takeover of Children's Cove and not the takeover

in SB the water's getting as dirty as Mission Bay
and the taquerias in the Funk Zone are suffering
Encinitas surfers underneath the golden domes
of SWAMI'S Keys in the velcro leashes and boards
Everything's hang loose here pants roomy and I'm
content as can be really the way that salt stays
and that satisfying full body tiredness hungover from

a sunburn and wave playing all that dredged
sand I'm going down to the POTATO SHACK
for starch and then heading over to LOU'S RECORDS
and the PANNIKIN to get coffee from a girl
with purple eyeliner even though I don't like
coffee Everything closes round eight p.m. and so
we'll watch the green flash or the red tide

Everyone's naïve and earnest Navy and New Age
Faux punk and smoothies not like the Bay
with its too much irony that isn't
The mayor was supposed to be a surfer not
this jackass Remembering making out in Stagecoach
Park on the jungle gym at night the middle of the
suburbs Going down to DAILY EXCHANGE in the
morning to buy some tight pants

Sandwiches

Charlie Daly

For now, I'll let the foam wash over my toes. Every ten minutes or so, a big set crashes. White water cascades toward the shore but stops before forcing me to higher ground. The sand is hot under my damp trunks. Beer cools my sun-chapped lips. It helps me forget that little will change before the sun dips below the water. I doubt my raw, peeling nose could get any redder, but the sun has time. She'll be just as gone when night falls and the trade winds die. I'll still have no way home. The waves will still pound the shore and run up my legs with the tide while I lie in the sand finishing our beers. She disappeared with my car while I swam in the surf. At least she realized I'd need the beer. The sun fries my eyelids while I try to sleep.

There's a hand on my chest.

"I got us some lunch. Did you miss me?" She kisses me and takes a seat in the sand. She hands me a sandwich wrapped in wax paper.

HUMAN SEEKING MEANING

Jennifer Brooke Williamson

is this it   the hearts in the wall   lets pretend time didn't   neck
exposed   don't be that   boys not my gender   slip of the cups
plastic to cement   one night   stare, look back   let's just be
scruffy sexy thing   tendency to over analyze   all could see
but   one of those   forced myself to risk   call back   something
to whine about   and yet   does it mean   hate these games
you just injured my   discomfort zone   exist   what's in your
head   too hard   i could never make   can't understand   a week
with the mark you left   won't call back   pressed to the   just
want you   mistaken connection?   one of those boys   it had
to be that   so nervous i could   must be   too many questions
awkward always   when two people collide

Lincoln Logs

Bill Peters

I first saw them on page one hundred twenty-two of the Sears Christmas Catalog. The picture showed houses and fences and forts, all built from simple wooden rods and slats. My brother and I could easily build a whole town with this set of Lincoln Logs. And when we were done we could wreck the whole thing. That would be the fun part—running a fist slowly through all the buildings and watching the wooden people tumble to the ground. This could be a great Christmas.

I showed the picture to my dad who nodded. "Pretty slick."

That did it. I took the catalog up to my room and started drawing more buildings in the margin—some houses, some stores and a jail. I drew a road that went between all the buildings and ended at the top of page one-twenty-three.

When my brother came home, he saw what I'd done and started drawing his own pictures. He surrounded the town with mountains and drew a Tyrannosaurus Rex behind the mountains. When one page was filled, we Scotch Taped another one to it and kept drawing. We made rivers with blue crayons that ran under bridges. We drew a forest at one end and a forest fire at the other end with lots of black smoke. We made cowboys and Indians, some lying dead with Xs where their eyes should be.

"Maybe the dinosaur can come over the mountains and into the town," my brother suggested.

"Okay, then the cowboys can attack it from one side and the Indians from the other side," I added. "That way he'd be trapped and killed."

On Christmas Eve we actually went to bed early so we could lie in our bunk beds and continue plotting.

"Maybe the dinosaur could get caught in the forest fire." I suggested.

My brother nixed that idea. "That's not bloody enough."

The next morning we came running downstairs and found the Lincoln Logs under the Christmas tree.

"Thanks, Santa," I shouted.

We got on our knees and started clearing a space on the living room carpet. We needed a fort first. Using a combination of logs connected in zigzag fashion, we created a large perimeter, big enough so we could both sit inside it. So far, so good.

But the scope of our plan had multiplied as we worked. We decided that the rest of the town would have to be built in the hallway and the dinosaur would probably come in from the back bedroom.

When we stood up to survey our progress, we both saw the problem. We each had one Lincoln Log left. We needed about seven hundred more.

Dad came in and observed with his hands on his hips. "How's it going?"

I gave my brother a frown at carpet level to discourage him from complaining about our predicament.

"Pretty good," I said. But the truth had sunk in. There wasn't going to be any outlaws or jails or battles with the dinosaur.

Mom called from the kitchen. "Clean that up now. It's time for breakfast."

We ate some oatmeal in silence, each thinking our own thoughts about what we were going to do next.

When we returned to the living room, my brother started picking up the Lincoln Logs and I got out the instruction book. Step by step we built a modest little house on a prairie of green carpet. It had a doorway and two windows and green slats for a roof.

My brother topped off the wooden house with a red wooden chimney. I took a short Lincoln Log and set it up right in front of the doorway. Our Pioneer. We folded all the plans we'd made and put them under the Lincoln Log box.

Mom came in from the kitchen and saw what we'd done.

"Did you build that all by yourselves?" She wiped her hands on a towel and leaned in to take closer look.

"Yup," we both said.

"You boys are truly amazing."

The Persistence of Memory

Oriana

A pigeon flew in through a window
on the fourth floor and got trapped
in the sheen of the long corridors
in the large building where we lived.

My father caught it and handed it to me.
I held the bird tight to my chest,
then leaned over the sill
and handed it to the sky.

For a moment it dropped, a dead
weight—then it wobbled,
the wings found again
the art of the air—

and the bird wheeled
above the wide yard. Flew away
like the years. But I still feel it beat,
that heart against my heart.

Once Upon a Time on Thursday

Amy Wolf

Sung Tae was still asleep. It was 3:36 when she had put him in his crib. Even though he could sleep undisturbed by the vacuum cleaner's churning motor, it was a wonder that he was still asleep after all the noise of the last twenty minutes. Maybe he was awake and she just hadn't heard his faint cry. She lay motionless on the living room floor, trying to detect any sound emanating from the back bedroom, but all she could hear were the scattered chirps of birds in the eucalyptus trees outside.

She knew she should get up, but she couldn't bring her body to move. She lay there for another twenty minutes, doing nothing but watching the shadows from the floor-length blinds wane in the diminishing afternoon sunlight. The birds continued to sing outside, first a timid call, then an entire chorus of loud replies.

Had it really been twenty minutes? Perhaps it was closer to fifteen or maybe even thirty? She had no way of knowing. She couldn't remember the exact time she had been pushed to the floor. She rolled to her left side, hoping to make out the electronic numbers on the VCR. 4:38. That meant that Sung Tae had been sleeping for an hour and two minutes which was the best thing that had happened all day. It was time to get up now; she knew for sure. If it was 4:38, it meant that Jae Sook would be back in thirty-seven minutes.

She had always been extremely aware of time, always able to accurately gauge the time to within two minutes if asked by a stranger on the street or a friend at a party. In high school, she had been her own pace clock, never needing to rely on the track coach to tell her that her third lap had been faster than the second lap, or that she had been off rhythm in the fourth lap. This internal measure of time, coupled with her long graceful stride was the reason she had excelled at running, her specialty the mile. She had long stopped running competitively, but she had kept that time-keeping gift until today, or more precisely, until this afternoon between 3:44 and 4:18, when she had lost her awareness of time.

Those thirty-four minutes were an exception to the rest of her life. She remembered the going-away party five months ago in a swanky hotel bar in Apujeong. Even though her girlfriends had thought their comments were confidential, she had heard their voices carry the length of the sleek black table.

"Kyeong Mi is so lucky. A perfect husband, a beautiful baby, and now moving to the United States! What a charmed life."

Although she could detect the underlying notes of jealously fueled by multiple rounds of soju shots, their comments did nothing to diminish her happiness.

But now she had the same luck as the sophomore girl in her university dormitory, the unfortunate one whose taxi driver had made a detour into a warehouse parking garage in the early hours of Sunday morning and committed unspeakable horrors. Whispers had traveled quickly up and down the dormitory halls. "What had she been doing out so late?" "What kind of girl was she?" "Would she come back to school?" Even Jae Sook had repeated those sentiments when she relayed rumors of the disgraceful incident to him.

She had grown up in a comfortable city just outside of Seoul with parents who doted on her throughout her childhood. She had an older sister who transitioned from favorite playmate into her closest confidante, freely offering encouragement and wisdom as she encountered the challenges of being a teenage girl. Her parents eagerly paid for their daughters to attend the best schools in the city, even if that meant a fifty-five minute bus ride each way by the time she was in high school. Besides academics, she had proven herself on the track field, culminating in plentiful awards and medals now carefully packed away in the far corners of a closet in her parents' apartment, along with other possessions that were deemed unworthy of the move to the United States.

She had been thrilled when she received the admissions notice to Seoul National University, one of the three best colleges in all of Korea. She had loved living in the city, loved it even more when she met Jae Sook, and had someone to accompany her on her Saturday subway trips around Seoul.

Their Saturday excursions stretched into Sunday breakfasts and Monday lunches, integrating their lives. This formation was finally announced to the world when Jae Sook placed a diamond ring on her finger the night before her college graduation. Within a few months, the diamond ring was joined by a simple silver band, its identical partner residing on the finger of her new husband.

In married life, time adopted a new dimension, each minute deepening in significance, each hour finishing with a satisfactory sense of wholeness, of nothing missing, of life being the way it was meant to be lived. She still indulged in lengthy runs through the city, patiently waiting in the elevator during its twenty-floor descent, then bounding out the half-open doors and away from the towering apartment complex into the hustle of the city's other ten million inhabitants. She expertly dodged lead-footed taxi drivers screeching around corners, and overflowing trash bags waiting to be erased from sight by perpetually late garbage collectors.

Thanks to their apartment's ideal location in the Yeouinaru district, she was running alongside the Han River within twenty minutes, never letting the buzz of traffic on overhead bridges or children flying kites in the park disrupt her stride. Head up, shoulders back, arms comfortably bent and moving at her sides, she ran the back half of the loop, navigating a string of side roads, ticking off landmarks in her mind—the house with the blue door, an almost-forgotten kimbap stand, a convenience store's neon sign—until she was hunched over outside her own apartment building, breathless from the final sprint.

She hadn't developed a running path in San Diego yet. The three months since the move had been filled with unpacking boxes, multiple trips to IKEA and Target to buy meager but functional furniture for their apartment, hanging framed photographs of family and friends that had survived the harsh journey across the ocean. These were the only traces of Korea in their apartment.

Living in the United States was a remarkable opportunity, the chance for Jae Sook to attend graduate school on a full fellowship, another ray of fortune blessing her and her small family, another gift of time to be spent pursuing new adventures.

She sat up slowly from the sturdy blue-green carpet, no doubt chosen by a previous tenant for longevity rather than style. Her husband's school, as part of the gracious fellowship offer, had arranged this two-bedroom apartment for them in the university's graduate student residence complex. The population was a mix of single American students, prone to festive gatherings in the middle of the week, and other foreign families like hers. Left to herself during the day, she had met a few other young Korean mothers as she pushed Sung Tae in his stroller, carefully tracing the sidewalk that ringed the spacious complex. It was the closest she had come to running these past months.

Her new friends welcomed her into their circle, all too aware of the challenges that came with living in the United States. They would gather in various apartments, sipping tea and sharing DVDs of Korean dramas. Occasionally, they would consolidate car seats into their assortment of used Hondas and Hyundais and caravan to the Asian grocery store. On the return trip, the cars filled with the pungent aroma of fresh kimchi and the bubbling sound of laughing voices singing along to Korean pop music.

Today had not been one of those days. Resting on the security of time, she had devised a daily schedule for herself within the first month. Thursday was divided between laundry, vacuuming, and as always, cooking that evening's dinner. This Thursday was marked by the unexpected ringing of the phone as she returned to the apartment, balancing the last basket of laundry on one hip and Sung Tae on the other. She had raced to unlock the door, pushed it closed with her foot and slid across the living room to grab the phone as it finished its sixth ring, forgetting to reach back and lock the door as she normally did.

After curtly ending the telemarketer's rehearsed speech, she had immediately launched into the vacuuming, gliding the machine in long strokes over the carpet. That effort had been futile, she now knew. The vacuum sprawled across the carpet in the far corner of the living room, wedged between the khaki twill couch and the pine coffee table, silent, its plug yanked from the outlet. He must have tripped over the cord when he snuck in, the toe of his scuffed, black Adidas sneaker pulling the cord until the tension snapped the plug from the wall outlet.

Sung Tae's faint wail echoed down the hallway as she rose to her feet. She walked swiftly to the small back bedroom, its floor peppered with the essentials of a nine-month-old. He sat patiently in his crib.

Returning to the front of the apartment, she surveyed the room as an outsider, still unsure how the events of the afternoon had occurred in this place. Except for the overturned vacuum cleaner and her pale blue underwear that lay carelessly by the leg of the coffee table, nothing seemed unusual.

But there was no time to dwell on that now. She returned the vacuum to the hall closet and shoved her underwear deep into the trash, past yesterday's leftover spaghetti, making sure to conceal the cotton fabric with an empty cereal box. Calculating efficiency against time expenditure, she settled for changing clothes instead of taking the long shower that she desperately desired. Fearing that the man's musky odor still lingered, she sprayed her wrists and neck with the lavender perfume that Jae Sook bought her when she was eight months pregnant, insistent that she never looked more beautiful than she did with her swollen belly.

Knowing that time was passing quickly, she worried she wouldn't be able to grasp the minutes required to cook dinner. She hoped that Jae Sook wouldn't mind eating a late dinner, that the undergraduates he taught on Thursday mornings hadn't upset him too much with their youthful chattiness and occasional lapse of studying, that he would be understanding when she told him. If she told him.

With Sung Tae happily ensconced in a playpen, she flung open cabinets, the hinge of the far left door squeaking in protest. Rice and water were unceremoniously dumped into the electronic rice maker in permanent residence on the crowded kitchen counter. Next to it, she cut green bell peppers on a white plastic cutting board. Flipping the board over, she carved thin slices of galbi, throwing both meat and vegetable into a sauce pan. Not noticing the rounded yellow-green numbers of the stove top's display as they slid effortlessly from 5:12 to 5:13 to 5:14, her rapid breathing matched the frenetic sizzling of the hot oil in the saucepan, popping and bursting louder and louder until she felt pressure on the small of her back: the warmth and strength of a man's hand.

She dropped the wooden spoon she held in her right hand and whirled around to look into Jae Sook's face, deep brown eyes glowing at her.

"I missed you," he said.

"I missed you, too." Her empty hand twitched and she averted her eyes from Jae Sook's to the floor, awkwardly bending down to pick up the spoon. She fidgeted as she stood up, aware that his gaze was still upon her.

"I love when you wear that lavender perfume. You should do it more often," he said.

"Dinner should be ready soon. I got started late."

"That's fine." Jae Sook bent down to kiss her lips then straightened and headed toward the playpen. With a shout of boyish glee, he swooped Sung Tae up and tossed him into the air, his capable arms easily catching and cradling seventeen pounds of baby. This father-son routine was completed over and over again. She watched them, trying to erase the awful image of that other man's angular face with greedy eyes and an arrogant jaw, the one who had entered her life just two hours ago. Detecting the scent of over-cooked beef, she turned her attention back to the night's dinner. She switched off the heat and piled tender galbi on top of steaming white rice, then brought small containers of kimchi, radish, and steamed tofu to the table.

Through the clank of metal chopsticks and slurping of tea, Jae Sook asked, "So, did you do anything interesting today?"

"Just laundry and vacuuming. How about you?"

"My seminar students were really good today. I think they're finally understanding the material." Sung Tae interrupted with a gurgle, spitting up part of his mashed sweet potatoes. She leaned toward his high chair, wet wipe in hand to attack the orangey mess. Jae Sook's eyes followed her as she walked from the table to the trash can to throw away the sticky tissue. His concentrated gaze extended beyond her, through the living room, out the floor-length window that formed one wall, and into the somber early evening dusk.

"How do you feel about living here?" he asked.

Her footsteps were slower on the way back to the table. Sinking into her high-backed wooden chair, she said, "It's nice enough. Why do you ask?"

"Some of the other Ph.D. students have heard rumors about a strange person wandering around this area. They don't think it's safe here."

She shrugged her shoulders. "I haven't noticed anything lately. It's always really quiet in these apartments. I never hear the neighbors."

While she usually valued privacy, she wished the apartment's sound-absorbing walls had collapsed that afternoon and allowed her cries of protest to ring out through the whole complex, down the street, and across the campus to her husband's cubicle halfway down a third-floor hallway in the engineering research center.

"So are you all right with living here?" he asked.

"We've just gotten settled. And I have friends close by. I don't want to leave them."

Sung Tae was drawing scribbled circles of sweet potato on the high chair's tabletop with his chubby fingers, which concluded his parents' conversation. Following their nightly routine, she bathed, changed, and dressed his little body, guiding pudgy limbs into pajama pants and sleeves. When she was confident that he was asleep, she slipped out of his bedroom, quietly making her way back toward the kitchen sink.

Jae Sook was already there, swishing a soapy sponge over the white plates with the red-striped rim. The tall cylinder glasses were upside down on a red kitchen towel next to the sink, a few remaining water drops dripping down into the absorbent cotton. She slid her slim body sideways between Jae Sook and the refrigerator to take a matching red towel out of a drawer and then circled behind him toward the half-dried dishes.

They worked in silence, having long ago lost the need to fill up every second spent together with words. She was drying the saucepan when she felt a drop of cold water land on her nose, the next sprinkling of even-colder water that fell across her cheeks and chest couldn't be ignored. She giggled softly, the ups and downs of her light voice mixing with the bass tones of Jae Sook's deep-hearted chuckle. More water was splashed and her towel swatted his backside. Then she was encapsulated in his arms, hers wrapped behind his back, each pulling the other closer. Then their lips were pressed together.

"Let's go to the bedroom," Jae Sook murmured.

Suddenly, she felt sick and drew her mouth away, afraid she might throw up. She remembered that she still hadn't taken a shower and then she could feel rough skin and hairy arms rubbing against her. She scratched her left forearm. Eyes downward, she replied, "Not tonight. I'm too tired."

Aware that if she looked at Jae Sook directly she would have to explain further, she slinked from the kitchen and sought refuge under the showerhead's jets of tepid water. She meticulously scrubbed every inch of her body, from her right pinky toe to the nape of her neck, wincing as the washcloth brushed over the bruises already forming on her forearms and thighs. After vigorously massaging her black hair with shampoo, she reached for the washcloth again not wanting to take any chances that she might have missed a spot.

The bathroom's steam was as opaque as her sense of time, both blocking the mirror's revelation of the truth. Feeling exposed while wrapped in her deep blue towel, she cautiously opened the bathroom door. She heard Jae Sook tapping his feet against the wooden chair leg, a twitch that always accompanied his studying She scurried for the empty bedroom. In the dark, she slipped on a pair of old running shorts and a faded tee shirt instead of one of the many dainty nightgowns both she and Jae Sook preferred.

She huddled under the feather comforter, tightly curled, shaking hands grasping bony knees, perched right up against the side of the bed as minute after minute crept by, her mind wide awake. When Jae Sook entered the room, softly pushing open the door, her body stiffened and she squeezed her eyes shut, hoping to project the appearance of sleep. Her ears followed his nightly routine: taking out tomorrow's clothes, draping them across the used plush armchair in the corner, neatly placing today's clothes in the wicker hamper in the back of the closet.

His footsteps grew closer and she felt a rush of cool air against her back as Jae Sook drew back the comforter to slide his own body into the warmth. He cautiously inched toward the middle of the bed until he was able to place his left hand on the curve of her left shoulder and lightly rub up and down her arm. Afraid the passage of time would erase any more chances for the truth, she rolled toward him without unwinding, letting her knees rest up against his chest.

"I have to tell you something," she said.

"It will be okay, Kyeong Mi. What is it?"

She whispered in his ear, her voice quivering as tears slid down her cheekbones, one after the other, in a parade of sorrow. Jae Sook just listened and then he hugged her, pulling her shaking body toward his until her head nestled in his bare chest and her tears ran directly over his heart. From the uncluttered nightstand beyond his shoulder, the clock's display glowed at her through the darkness. It was 10:08.

THIS FEAR OF FALLING

Lauren Wilensky

she stands on the rickety wooden bridge,
a century before her birth it collapsed,
villagers tell the tragic story,
they found carriages of people splintered,
floating against the river current,

never completely cleaned-up,
instilled remnants
under the obsidian rocks,
on the muddy flanks of the riverbed,
next to the hoofed ground of oak trees.

her doctors found lung cancer,
cradled in pink-toned pockets
of dead muscle,
                warped, raw, ash stained to black,
the surgeons dove into her body.

she stands against the bridge
waiting for it to break, the strength
in her legs   the ledge,
tumbling
down soft
like snow flakes
and she forgot   they said,
snow falls harder these days.

Fighting for Light

Tori Malcangio

Lisa thought Steve could have passed for an extra in a John Mellencamp video—the way he sat in his leatherette recliner, his old Martin guitar, a faded John Deere tee shirt, pieces of weekend mulch burrowed in his arm hair. He was practicing the pentatonic scale in A, warming up for tomorrow.

The guitar was about a decade old, hardly used in the last three years, except the few Sundays he resurrected it to show Eli, their two-year-old son, what a man looked like with music on his mind: one leg propped up on the guitar case, eyes shut, then open, to watch fingers blaze red at the tips.

After Lisa put Eli to bed, she watched Steve from the kitchen; his vice-grip on the rosewood body as if to keep from losing it to a thief. Frenetic fingers flying up and down the fret board, outpacing his thoughts. Ten resolute minds dancing to a song he'd first heard on the radio when he was French kissing Lisa, before the tongue and ape-shit abandon had become a novelty.

When Lisa first met him, Steve could play anything by ear. They sat up some nights writing terrible rhyming couplets and drinking equally unpalatable wine. He sang, she danced, and somewhere in the buzz of it all they ended up on top of his white sheets, her long brown hair spread across his cheap polyester pillows like an alluvial fan. And then he lost it—not the ear—the I-don't-give-a-shit attitude required to keep at something despite the overwhelming odds of it ever being heard.

The playing started again yesterday after the phone call from Steve's uncle.

"Steve, Uncle Les here. What you think 'bout giving your dad's eulogy tomorrow?"

"Honestly, Les, not up for it," Steve said. "I can play something. Something real nice on the guitar. I'm no speech giver. Besides, Dad wasn't big on them."

"Don't make no difference to me—words or music, music or words. Your dad ain't going to hear nothing anyway." Les sipped something, chuckled. "You can play the guitar?"

"Since I was seven."

"Well, hell then, play Steve-O. Your dad never mentioned you being a music man."

Lisa studied moths fighting for first rights to the patio light. Listen: dusted wings clipping, soft bodies bumping. She jumped when the air conditioning clicked on. The cool air lifted pieces of Steve's hair. He batted at them, as if his dad had shown up to intervene, to suggest baseball or soccer or *a goddamn big boy's game*. In between scales Lisa kissed Steve goodnight.

"I'm heading up to read."

"Stay," he pleaded.

"Hon, I can hear you from upstairs. You're my soundtrack."

He wanted her close enough to hear her applaud, should he happen to arrive at miraculous. When she was in the same room, when her hair was close enough to smell, her breathing audible, he was better for it.

"Where should I stand tomorrow?" he asked, his voice thin as used-up guitar strings. "At the casket, or keep my distance? Is it bad form to play when someone can't ask you to stop?"

"Play and I'll tell you. I'll be honest," she said.

Lisa sat at his bare feet. As his fingers broke the first notes of "Hotel California," his mouth slacked open and complicated bits of boyhood escaped—some malignant masses, some mere antidotes of a father who had tried, but failed.

At *this could be heaven or this could be hell* his white knuckles regained red, his left foot tapped tempo again. She watched his rigid body syncopate a thousand contrary rhythms until he seemed to be reconciling a father's debts and his own empty vaults. Refrain by refrain, she watched him replace fury with forgiveness, as if warming up to show Eli how to peel a banana, or toss seaweed back into the ocean, or capture a moth and let it go.

Letter Found in a Cave

Seretta Martin

When on a stroll, if you meet a galloping herd of feathered horses with copper mouths snapping open and shut, resist the urge to kneel before them offering sugar. I say this to protect you. I could say nothing, but I care for you more than you want. In the forest at night silver frogs make a blessed bellowing, deep and low, like a draft on open flames. I welcome the hollow sound of gunmetal sky. I add one further thought to you, a question rather. Does the water flow uphill in your country too?

(I don't remember reading about it) I'm writing to you from the end of the last day.

Here, the stars burn a hole in the sky; space between them is narrowing beyond.

No one knows why. There's little for us to focus on and we have lost sight of the wind.

Mother and Son

Al Zolynas

Jonas had celebrated his eleventh birthday the previous Friday. His mother now referred to him as her "little man," something which both pleased and embarrassed him.

She now expected more from him, she said, as she showed him how to darn his own socks. (He already knew how to iron shirts and pants, covering the woolen slacks with a wet handkerchief to bring the creases out better.) He held a sock over the loosely-made fist of his left hand, the hole in the sock's big toe over the circle made by his thumb and forefinger. With needle and thread, he cross-hatched across the gaping hole just as his mother was doing with one of his father's socks. It was, he thought, like the kind of cross-hatching he did with his pencil when he wanted to represent shading in one of the drawings he was always doing—and it was almost as pleasurable.

His mother looked over at him across the gray Formica kitchen table and complimented him on his progress.

When he finished, the darned hole looked like a healed-over scar. The sock was hardly like new again, but still there'd be a new bit of soft wool for his toe to nestle into. He felt a sense of accomplishment, of having done something worthy. It fulfilled his sense of order and craft and even art. Not quite the same as the satisfaction he got from painting water colors at his school in weekly art class or of making a papier-mâché hand puppet—but definitely a good feeling.

Another good feeling came when he pulled the restored sock onto his bare foot and felt the new sensation on his big toe, drawing attention to the absolute fact of its existence. It was as if the darned hole was now literally a scar on his toe and that his toe was bigger and his foot somehow grown beyond itself.

Jonas's mother rose from the table, poured water into the kettle, lit the stove, and brewed them tea. They drank it European-style: strong with sugar and a slice of lemon each. He loved how the lemon lightened the color of the tea to a bright amber and how, when he stirred, it floated and turned slowly on the surface like a little yellow wagon wheel, or, as you and I might say had we been there, like a mandala.

They sipped their tea. The house was quiet. It was the 1950s in suburban Australia, and quiet was something that still existed then. It was taken for granted, though loved and revered nonetheless. The refrigerator clicked on and began to whir, which only deepened the essential and primordial silence.

Jonas and his mother each took another holey sock from the pile and slipped them over their fists, and it occurred to Jonas to ask his mother why they were mending the socks of his dead father, but in the next moment he was sure he knew the answer.

A Mix-up

Jess Jollett

I forgot I wasn't a lesbian. I forgot that I was a pastor's daughter who likes boys. Boys with brown eyes, in football jerseys and pickup trucks. But Trisha had short hair and doe eyes. And it could have been the tequila or that horrible Blur song they played about boys and girls. Or maybe it was that nipple. It looked like tortoise shell double-breasted buttons on my favorite winter coat. Or a sand dollar you discover by sifting sand with toes. Like that patty of meat sizzling on the grill the last summer my father and I agreed.

A Snail Kingdom

Eber Lambert

Not long ago I was driving to work in morning drizzle and a cumulus mood, when I came to a section of road covered with lug nut-sized rocks. The distribution was migratory: the formation emerging from the landscaped slope on the right side of the road and tapering into a point a couple yards from the other shoulder. I slowed the car to a rolling stop when it suddenly dawned on me: These weren't rocks, they were snails. Hundreds of snails that had forsaken the sheltered life of the moist ice plant on the eastern embankment to march with their fellow snails unwisely into the westbound lane of Carmel Valley Road.

Their exodus was not without tragedy. A pair of tire tracks, poorly retraced by several cars, sliced across the triangular horde, leaving two swaths of a pulverized slurry of dead and mortally wounded for the other snails to climb over or through or, in several cases, to stop to snack on. Nonetheless, the rank and file soldiered on—sluggishly you might say. But why?

Perhaps it was innate snail curiosity, the lure of the great frontier that led to heroic exploration beyond their known world, a goal of colonization, of transcendent bounty that they calculated would exist on the other side. Or perhaps they were driven by a higher power; one that would crush their aspirations and punish them for this quest of self-determination, since in another ten or twelve feet they would discover that the promised land beyond their mollusk horizon was desolate and uninhabitable, nothing but seared desert rubble and sparse chaparral. They were utterly doomed and had no way of knowing it.

Maybe they unwisely chose to follow a deranged snail leader—a Judas Escargot—or a politically connected cabal that had decided it was time to put pod to the asphalt and blindly lead the once stable snail nation to almost certain catastrophic demise. Perhaps the ice plant Shangri-la had become overpopulated due to its remote location and a dearth of the snails' natural predator—the homeowner, those unfeeling giants with their poisons and huge feet, who are often compelled to throw innocent snails at a nearby wall, fence, or, for the true sportsman, a tree trunk or utility pole.

Could it be that the cultural stagnation and despair in the ice plant had become unbearable? This could be an irrational or even deliberate mass suicide by an ignorant civilization too stupid to grapple with the harshness of reality, rather than the misguided wholesale slaughter of social progress gone horribly awry.

One can only hope that after this apocalyptic chapter, a few remaining gastropods would retreat back to a kinder, gentler ice plant, begin to rebuild a new world based on reason and prudence, eschewing superstition and megalomania, and resisting the urge to venture beyond their intellectual abilities ever again. Snails must learn their limitations, teach their young to appreciate and take care of the ice plant, not to overpopulate and foul their environment, not to follow incompetent leaders, or blindly accept bogus prophecies or unfounded speculation. Or else they, and thousands after them, will end up once again on the rapidly warming asphalt waiting to burn in the midday sun or be destroyed by invincible powers they can neither see nor comprehend.

In a moment of reverence and cosmic authorization, I put the car into gear rolling forward to cut a new set of genocidal tracks through the languid multitude, making sure my driver's side tires crushed those on the point leading the way.

Musings of the Tin Man

Clifton King

What was it mother said: never
play near a recycling center
or insult a man carrying a can opener.

It's not like life was easy before WD40,
what with all that salt they toss across
the yellow brick road every winter.

And my uncle talks of times he
and my aunt Lizzy vacationed
at the shore, how he rubbed her down
with 30 weight Pennzoil, polished
her back side with a Brillo pad.

Yet, later in life when the rust
refused to be rebuffed
she had zerk fittings installed.

And of course my grandfather's
tales of his brother the rusty Buick,
my cousins the sardine cans.

Yes, I know, I'm not proud of it,
but you can't choose your relatives.

Now, here I stand caught in the rain,
rust stains swirling around my ankles,
me without an umbrella or K-Y Jelly.

I should have stayed home, enjoyed
a nice warm cup of Liquid Wrench.
I should have listened to Mother.

VERACITY

William Cass

I had no intention of becoming a school administrator. My old principal, who'd been sort of like a second mother, recommended me to a local university on some form that came across her desk. The college contacted me and I went. As an elementary school teacher, one's career options are limited. I'd intended to go back for my MA anyway, for no more lofty reason than moving up the salary scale, so I figured I might as well get it in something that at least had a future application.

Then the summer school principal-thing came up, so I'd agreed to that for a few years after my regular teaching term ended. Among our largely well-to-do, demanding parent population, the program was much more involved and more closely scrutinized than others elsewhere. This was a community where my wife and I could not afford to rent, let alone own a home. My old principal said that summer school was just a microcosm of the regular school year, complete with myopic reasoning, over-zealousness, and remarkable incapacity for taking responsibility for oneself. In short, as she once described things, the sort of place where people were born on third base and thought they'd hit a triple.

So, there were problems. That was a given. But most of the major ones were dealt with before the summer session began or during its first couple of days, and the month of classes normally progressed smoothly. It had the first two years I held the position, as well as that particular summer, in spite of Julia Denaldi and her husband.

She was waiting to see me after the third day of classes. I was out in front for longer than usual, waiting for a father who was late coming to pick up his son. By the time I got back, the office was mostly empty. Jean, our school secretary, discreetly pointed her out, sitting on the sofa flipping though a glossy picture book with her daughter. Jean mouthed the words, "pain in the ass," and I remembered her description of the woman at registration, a former classmate of hers, who had apparently grown up in a big house across from the ocean. She rolled her eyes and left through the front door.

I went up to the two of them and said, "Hello. I'm the summer school principal. Can I help you with something?"

"I'm Julia DeNaldi and this is Aubrey," the woman said. She gazed at her daughter, who I supposed was about the same age as my own, with a lingering smile. I noticed that the woman's skin was a shade of brown only nurtured through careful diligence but that her daughter's was naturally dark.

"Hello, Aubrey," I said, and we smiled at each other.

"Aubrey has been in the Montessori pre-school program for the past two years," Mrs. DeNaldi began. "It's a marvelous program, as I'm sure you know. However, her placement here so far has been less than satisfactory. Frankly, she's bored. I'd like to move her to another class."

I felt my shoulders stiffen and asked, "Which class is she in?"

"Mrs. Fuentes' Introduction to Kindergarten," she said.

I looked over their heads out the window and thought about what I was hearing: a complaint regarding a four-year-old who had yet to make her first official step into a public school classroom. Our custodian, Frank, was taking in the cones that lined the car pickup lane, a lane people mostly ignored. I liked Frank. Normally, I would be out helping him with the cones. He smiled and waved.

I looked back at the two of them on the couch and said, "Listen. It's the third day. Our entire program is only twenty school days long. We stay away from switching kids in classes. Give it some more time, and I'm sure the class will work out fine for you. Mrs. Fuentes is a highly regarded regular-year teacher."

"Oh, I like her," Mrs. DeNaldi said. "I like her fine. It's a control issue. It's a stimulation issue. Or lack thereof on both counts, to be more precise. She doesn't engage Aubrey. I don't believe she speaks directly to Aubrey a half-dozen times a day. Does she, hon?"

The little girl looked up at her mother and shrugged, then flipped the page in her book.

Mrs. DeNaldi went on. "I also feel strongly that her particular room lacks adequate peer challenge for Aubrey."

I felt my color begin to rise. I said, "I believe the challenge in Mrs. Fuentes' room to be developmentally sound. I have a daughter myself in that class."

Mrs. DeNaldi sighed. "I've been by Julie Bennett's classroom and have noticed that a worksheet is set out each day on all the desks when the students arrive. And I've talked with other mothers. The distinction seems quite clear."

I glanced outside deliberately and counted slowly to five. As a regular-year teacher myself, I could only guess how many times my principal had received comments like this about me. I watched Frank fit the last two cones onto his cart. Then I looked at Mrs. DeNaldi. Her green eyes were fixed steadily on me. I supposed she was about my age, forty or so.

I said, "I'm afraid what you've told me is unfortunate. Despite what you might think or have discussed with others, both teachers we're speaking of are equally fine instructors. I'm going to respectfully request that you not make judgments based on looking in classroom windows or reputations loosely formed on the street among parents. Neither is appropriate or accurate."

Mrs. DeNaldi sat very still. I watched her chest rise and fall under her expensive linen blouse. Finally, she said, "My husband commands a Navy Seal team. Are you aware of that?"

I said, "I guess I am now."

She said, "Yes. Well, he's out training at the moment. He'll be back soon."

"Fine," I said. It came out more suddenly than I'd intended. "Well, then, I hope you both have a good holiday weekend."

I walked quickly into my office and around the corner where I couldn't be seen. I heard the front door open and close. It was foolish, but I was trembling and couldn't understand why. A few moments later, I heard Frank come inside, set his cart against the wall, and go back out front. As the door shut again, I closed my eyes.

It was the Wednesday before the long July Fourth weekend. My wife, daughter, and I headed up to the eastern side of the Sierras for a short backpack trip out of Onion Valley for the weekend. The weather was fine. We didn't catch any fish at the lake where we camped, but we day-hiked up into some smaller lakes over the pass and hooked a few nice brown trout. My daughter caught her first ever, almost ten inches, on the same lure that had skunked me the previous two hours. We spent a lot of time around the campfire, slept late, identified wildflowers, had a nice time.

Mrs. DeNaldi didn't come around Monday, but she was there on Tuesday at mid-morning. When I returned from the playground after recess, she and her daughter were sitting straight-backed on the sofa in the exact same spot where I'd left them the previous week. This time, both were looking out the window. Mrs. DeNaldi's mouth was set in a thin line and she was twisting a gold necklace around her neck.

Jean raised her eyebrows when I came in, but frankly, I'd been expecting them at some point. I'd gone over what I thought I might say while I cooked dinner each night at our campsite and my wife and daughter recited nursery rhymes.

I took a breath, went up to them, and asked if I could help them.

Mrs. DeNaldi said, "We need to talk."

I showed them into my office and closed the door. We sat down around a table in the corner. Mrs. DeNaldi exhaled deeply as if to unburden herself of a great weight. She said, "We gave it a fair chance. We did. I like Mrs. Fuentes personally, but she has no control. Aubrey is learning nothing. She comes home in tears. She doesn't want to come to school. I would prefer, no, I *want* to have her changed to Julie Bennett's class."

I nodded and looked at the little girl. I said, "How are you, Aubrey?"

She said, "Good."

"My daughter, Katie, says she likes playing with you on the playground. She says you chase each other."

Aubrey smiled. She said, "But we don't go up the slide the wrong way with our feet."

"I know that," I said quietly. "Thank you for using the slide safely."

A truck stopped outside in front of the school. I looked out the window at the warehouse guy bringing our supply order early because one of our first grade teachers needed crepe paper for a project she was doing. I wanted to be out there to acknowledge his extra effort and to thank him.

Instead, I found myself saying, "Here's our policy on changing classes: we don't do it. You're interested in switching classes because you prefer one teacher to another. The curriculum is the same in each, as is the quality of instructor. We don't change placements during the regular year, nor do I have the latitude to do it during summer school." I had no idea if this last statement was true or not; I was only playing at the administrator role for a couple of months each year. "So we won't do it," I went on. "I'm sorry."

Mrs. DeNaldi was shaking her head, her eyes narrow. She looked at me as if I was pathetic. She said, "So, what you're telling me is that putting her in Ms. Bennett's class is not an option, in spite of the fact that I'm paying taxes for this program?"

I nodded. I'd planned on making a point about what her daughter would learn or not learn about life from this, but knew that if I said more, I would lose my temper. As it was, my voice had already been shaking a little.

Mrs. DeNaldi's eyes had nearly closed. What she said next came out through clenched teeth. "On three separate occasions, I've heard Mrs. Fuentes speaking Spanish to students and parents. Distinctly. Both before school and at dismissal. This is an American school. We're not in Mexico."

I stood up then. As evenly as I could, I said, "We're done here."

"Come, Aubrey," Mrs. DeNaldi hissed. She stood up and took her daughter by the hand. "Let's go."

I didn't walk them out. I sat down at my desk and typed at my laptop. I knew that the clerical staff had watched them leave and then turned their attention to me through the open door. I pretended to type for a few more minutes, then went back out to the playground where I'd promised a phys ed teacher I'd help umpire a kickball game for him.

I didn't see Aubrey or her mother again for the remainder of the session. I wasn't sure if they'd dropped out of the program or not; no news was good news, as far as I was concerned.

There weren't any other real problems of note after that for the last few weeks. Just the regular variety of challenges. Someone had broken some tree branches near the cafeteria over a weekend, so I helped Frank with that after classes one day. We had an ugly custody situation that I finally had to call the judge about: a dad wanted to take his son and daughter a weekend before his visitation rights really began. A little girl got her knee stuck between the bars of the big toy; she became hysterical, but some soap suds and soothing from the nurse finally did the trick. Another little boy missed two weeks because of a broken arm. There were also phone calls to make regarding misbehavior, a tricky facility deep-cleaning schedule to organize, and the like.

After the last day of the session, most of the teachers met at a local microbrewery to celebrate. I was late because I wanted to clear the office staff of their responsibilities so they wouldn't have to come in the next day. By the time I got to the place, it was after six, and the mood was on the gradual and happily graceful decline from festive. Contentment and relief were in the teachers' faces: vacation had begun.

The party took place on the back patio. Someone handed me a glass of beer when I walked up, and several made affectionately glib comments about my late arrival. People were talking and laughing quietly in small groups. Lydia Fuentes' husband, who taught fifth grade with me during the regular year, was sitting on a tall stool in the corner strumming a guitar. Two women who taught first grade stood next to him trying to ad lib the words to the song he was playing. A spray of bougainvillea burst lustily over the latticed fencework above them.

Lydia came over to me and said, "Well, how do you feel? Glad it's over?"

"Sure. You?"

She nodded emphatically. "You bet. Are you all finished, though?"

"Basically. I have a few things to do in the morning. Some forms to fill out for the state, some furniture to get moved, that's it."

"Well," she said, "you did a great job."

"So did you. My daughter loved being in your class."

"Katie is a sweetheart. She's a doll. I hope I get her in the fall."

"That would be wonderful," I said. But I felt a little guilty saying it because over the course of the session, it seemed that her class did lack some control and direction. She came running in most mornings at the last minute and often appeared to be winging things. Several times, Katie had come home and cheerfully announced that they'd watched cartoons on television.

"I wish they could all be as easy as Katie," Lydia said. "But unfortunately, that's not the case." She gestured with her head. "Speak of the devil."

I looked through the window and saw an olive-skinned naval officer in a khaki uniform slap his hand on the bar and laugh loudly. Two other officers stood at the bar with him laughing, too. They were in the far corner near the open doorway where they were apparently allowed to smoke the cigars they were holding.

"Have you met him?" Lydia asked. "I'm sure you've met his wife, the delightful Mrs. D."

"That Mr. D.?"

"Lieutenant DeNaldi," Linda corrected. "On the fast track to admiral, according to his wife."

I watched Lieutenant DeNaldi blow a stream of smoke at the ceiling.

"So, did you?" Lydia asked. "Deal with Mrs. DeNaldi?"

"We spoke a couple of times."

"I thought so. Thanks for whatever you said. She stopped spying through the window."

"I thought she stopped coming around altogether."

"They both did, mostly. She did show up once last week and brought Aubrey and her little cousin. She asked if the cousin could stay, too. I probably should have run it by you, but I didn't want to make a big deal over it, so I said sure. I'm certain Mrs. DeNaldi and her sister just needed someone to babysit while they went to Nordstrom or the beach or whatever."

One of the officers raised two empty pitchers and called to the bartender. The shadows outside were beginning to lengthen. Inside, a waitress was lighting the butterscotch-colored glassed candles on the tables with a fireplace match.

"Aubrey did come today for the final party," Lydia said. "Of course, she insisted on being first in line for treats and cried when she wasn't. Threw a little hissy fit."

One of our computer lab teachers banged on his mug with a spoon and called for a toast. He toasted summer, summer everywhere, summer evenings in particular. Before people could drink, Lydia's husband called him a poet and toasted poetry, especially poetry in the souls of the young. Lydia toasted restraint, particularly the restraint and discretion I'd shown that summer. People clapped and I stood to toast them. I tried to think of something clever to say, but I could only think of the word: veracity. So, I toasted that in them. Everyone laughed, and our remedial reading teacher toasted vocabulary and vocabulary development. Her teaching partner rose then and toasted a language arts adoption with a decent vocabulary development component. Lydia's husband began playing "Summertime Blues," and people clapped and sang along. I slipped away and walked through the bar to the restroom.

When I came out, Lieutenant DeNaldi was standing in front of the restroom door with his hands on his hips.

I stopped and he said, "Tom DeNaldi. I have something to say and it's this: I don't appreciate the way you treated my wife and daughter. Not a bit. In fact, it stinks. In fact, it pisses me off a lot."

I said, "I'm not sure what you're talking about."

"I think you do. I'm a public servant, too. My job is to serve the damn public. That's supposed to be your job, as well." He spat into a corner. "That's what I think of your public serving."

He'd left his drink and cigar on the corner of the bar nearby. We looked one another in the eye; his full of drink and anger. He was a short man with a broad chest. His two friends were standing against the bar smiling and watching silently.

I said, "I'm pretty sure you don't have the full story. Let's leave it at that."

"No," he said, "we won't leave it at that. I just got back from Washington yesterday. Had I been around earlier, I would have come down to that school of yours and we would have spoken. Or more to the point, I would have spoken and you would have listened."

We looked some more at one another. He stood closer, a dark-haired man with a handsome, closely-shaven face. I could smell the beer and cigar. "All right," I said as calmly as possible. "Consider it duly noted."

I walked past him, around the bar, and back outside to the patio. No one there looked up at me. I sat at the long table and ate a carrot stick. Everyone was still singing. I glanced across the street at the donut shop my daughter and I came to sometimes on Saturday mornings before we drove over to the boat harbor to feed the ducks.

A waitress came out and I signaled to her. I'd intended to buy a round for everyone, so I did that. I stayed until they were well into those drinks before I excused myself, wished everyone a wonderful rest of the summer, and left.

I walked around the corner to the parking lot, listening to the crickets, and opened my car door. I wasn't quite inside when I heard a grunt and looked across the lot where Tom DeNaldi was loosening the lug nuts on his back driver-side tire, which was flat. I straightened up and watched him take the spare out of his trunk and toss it behind the car. Then he fished through his trunk some more, stood up empty-handed, kicked the bumper, and swore. He put his hands on his hips, gazed back into the trunk, and swore again louder.

I looked away from him to the apartments across the alley. There was no one else in the parking lot. I closed my eyes and shook my head. Then I went to the back of my car, took the jack out of the trunk, and walked over to him. He was still standing with his hands on his hips, his back to me, staring into the trunk.

I said, "Looks like you could use this." He turned around. I held the jack with both hands. "I think it'll work. It's not from a BMW, but it's a pretty generic model."

He didn't say anything for a moment. I could hear a baseball game coming from a TV or radio through one of the open apartment windows. Finally, he said, "My wife bought this car while I was out to sea this winter. She must have got it without checking for a damn jack."

I nodded and knelt down next to the flat tire. I felt under the frame for the notch, found it, and wound the jack until it met the frame. The car began to rise. It didn't fit perfectly, but the blacktop was flat, and I knew it would work fine.

He knelt down next to me when the tire was off the ground and replaced it with the spare. I held it straight while he finger-tightened the lug nuts. Then I lowered the jack, slipped it out, and put his flat tire in his trunk while he cinched down the nuts with the tire iron. He seemed to take a long time doing it. A line of sweat was spreading along his backbone through his pressed uniform.

Finally, he stood up, leaving the tire iron on the ground and wiping his hands together. He stood looking at his hands.

"You going to be all right?" I asked.

"I think so," he said. "Sure." He looked into the trunk, I thought, to be looking anywhere but at me.

"Just so you know," I said, "my daughter enjoys playing with yours at the municipal pool. They have a good time there together."

He turned around and narrowed his eyes at me. "Your daughter a little blonde-haired girl with a round face?"

I nodded.

"She there yesterday afternoon with your wife? Wearing a green baseball cap?"

I nodded some more.

"I was throwing them those rings that sink to the bottom. They were diving for them."

The light had fallen towards evening and there was the slight fragrance of jasmine that came with it. I knew our paths had little chance of crossing again. If they did, we'd avoid talking. That much was for certain. Somewhere nearby a dog barked.

He said, "I think I owe you one of those juice boxes then. Your daughter gave mine one. How about I buy you a drink instead?"

"No," I said. "Thanks, though."

We didn't shake hands. I walked over to my car, put the jack inside, and left the parking lot. I didn't look back to see if he was still there. Instead, I drove for a while and thought about the next day. If I got up early, I could finish at school by lunch. Then I hoped to have time to weed the garden before we left for the airport. We were going to northern Montana where my wife's family had a lake cabin out in the woods. It was a place where you could listen to the lake lap softly at the shore in the evening, or an owl back in the trees late at night, where you could paddle over to one of the islands in the canoe for a picnic or to spend the night under the stars, a place where you could swim to the creek to see if there were any frogs on the flat rocks there.

The street I usually turned on that led to the freeway was blocked off for construction so I drove up the alley next to it instead. At the end of the alley, I was surprised to see Mrs. DeNaldi turning the key to the front door of a cottage. Aubrey was at her side. It was one of those alley places that used to be servants' quarters a long time ago but had been turned into a rental. A little wooden cottage in need of paint with a red scooter like my daughter's tipped over on the front walk. It wasn't much of a place. A pretty big step down from where she'd grown up across from the beach. But even a naval officer's salary wouldn't go far in that town. A little blush laced with chagrin crept over me. I thought of waving but by that time I was passing their place, and they'd both gone inside.

Then I was on the freeway with a breeze blowing in the window, and concentrated again on the lake and getting up early with my daughter and hiking to the falls to pick huckleberries and wildflowers. I smiled. It was something we loved to do. In fact, when she couldn't sleep during the winter, I often lay next to her in her bed and whispered to her about it.

47 Book Titles from My-Shelf

Gerald Vanderpot

Gerald's Game <u>of</u> Words Worth:

A Fan's Notes <u>on</u> Blue Highways <u>and</u> Pure Baseball

Under The Perfect Sun The Time is Noon <u>for</u> The Power of Blackness

The Case of Joe Hill <u>is</u> A Day of Light and Shadows

The Grapes of Wrath Makes Me Wanna Holler, "The Earth and Its People <u>are</u> Leagues Apart!"

Sons of Human Bondage <u>to</u> Poor Workers Unions <u>are</u> Beyond the Melting Pot

Raise High the Roof Beam <u>a</u> Strategy for Labor

Faithful Son of the Revolution <u>is</u> Beneath the Wheel

Rabbit, Run Beyond Good and Evil

"Leave Your Mind Behind The Door," The City Boy Secrets Howl

Beat Generation So Long, See You Tomorrow

All You Need is Love, <u>a</u> Woodstock Vision, <u>is</u> The Future of the Past

Bob Dylan, The Mayor of McDougal Street, <u>was</u> Bound for Glory

Suddenly, The Subterraneans <u>are</u> Good Enough to Dream <u>in</u> The Americans['] Armed Madhouse

From Bauhaus to Our House, A People's History of the United States <u>or</u> How I Found America <u>by</u> Abe and Me

Dirty Laundry

Celeste Carpenter

They were bright pink with white lace, and I could tell they'd been worn. I'd found them stuffed in the front pocket of his jeans, and now the underwear lay at my feet with the rest of the dirty laundry. I searched our apartment and found one of his dress shirts with makeup on the collar balled up and stuffed in the back of his closet, a pair of panty hose tucked inside. That night, he called to say he'd be working late again, so I arranged what I'd found on the couch, curled up in the chair with a bottle of red wine, and waited.

It was dark when I awoke, and my mind was dizzy from the alcohol. I uncurled my stiff legs and stared out into the edgeless room.

"I have a confession," said a woman's voice, high and raspy like she'd spent all night in a smoky bar.

My heart leapt in my throat, and I re-tasted the peanut butter sandwich I'd had earlier. Digging my fingers into the chair's arms to steady myself, I could just see the silhouette of a large woman sitting on the edge of the couch, her head tilted toward me.

Is it her? Is the bitch in my house! My anger grew, eclipsing my fear.

"I know you've been sleeping with my husband," I spit out with less force than I'd wanted.

"Yes, you're right I have, but there's more," answered the voice in a deep whisper, something familiar now traveling in the words.

Have we met before? My mind, racing through all of the women my husband knew, suddenly froze as she turned on the lamp, closing the space between us, and I stared at my husband's shimmery pink lips as he wiped a tear from a face not his.

"You see, my love, I've been sleeping with you as well."

Bufo

Steve Kowit

Up here in the high desert after the rains,
the bug-eyed toad bounces up out of nowhere
& starts hopping around like some sort
of goblin or sprite, this fellow who's leapt
out in front of my feet, all warty & shining
& bloated—this squat, cocky Bufo boreas,
hunkering now on a rock by the aloes, his thorax
throbbing away. Where on earth did he come from?
How did he manage to get here now
that the longed-for rains are upon us—
sitting up on that rock with the look of one
who has something to tell, one who's
been sent for, one who'd been looking
for someone like me, as much as to say
if I'd drop to my knees in the wet grass
& gaze up at his vast, bulbous, oracular eyes,
I would learn at long last—ah, but the chap
has in fact already hopped off & is bouncing
his way thru the muck like one who's already
delivered his message & has errands
no doubt as urgent for others. God knows
where he's headed. As for me, it would,
I believe, be circumspect just to keep
walking down to the shed as if nothing
the least bit untoward had occurred, making
my way thru the glorious puddles & mud
now that the longed-for rains at last are upon us!

The Fracture

Judy Goldstein Botello

Rosa Navarro was eighty-two years old, frail as a sparrow, but she could still impress my teenage son with her vigorous sit-ups. She had spent her childhood in Zacatecas, a small city in central Mexico, during the turbulent and romantic years of the Mexican Revolution; her eyes still flashed when she told of watching from behind her mother's skirts as Pancho Villa swept into town with his men. By the time she had graduated from Normal School the fighting had abated, and she served the new revolutionary government of Mexico as an itinerant teacher, traveling by burro to remote villages where she brought the gifts of literacy and hope to the peasants. Decades after her retirement she was still addressed respectfully as *Maestra*, and neighborhood children still came to her door for a cup of chocolate and a reading lesson. Long before the women's movement she had embraced single motherhood, raising my husband and his brother alone, with dignity and pride.

Like some migratory bird, she flew north each spring from her home near Mexico City to spend a few months with us in California. While here, she would amuse herself knitting woolen slippers for every member of the family or preparing herbal remedies for my occasional attacks of the blues, which Rosa cheerfully called *"los nervios."* But she was happiest on those occasions when we would take her to see the San Diego Padres play baseball. Then she would rise to her full five feet and sing the national anthem proudly, in a fine vibrato, although the words she sang were all of her own invention.

The day she broke her hip she was en route to us but had stopped to visit a sister in Ensenada, seventy miles south of the San Diego–Tijuana border. The phone call came from Ensenada one bright June morning while I was at my office in San Diego's Children's Hospital. In a frightened voice my husband's cousin, Sara, poured out a jumbled message: Rosa had fallen, they took her to the hospital, the doctors were talking surgery, we must come right away. My mind swarmed with images: Rosa humming in my kitchen as she prepared the world's best *albondigas*; Rosa guiding me through the vibrant maze of a Mexican market; and a future image of Rosa diminished, moving painfully from bed to bathroom with a walker as I had seen so many elderly patients do. My voice was shaking as I reassured Sara that we would be there as soon as possible.

The Social Security Hospital in Ensenada is an old one-story structure huddled between a paint store and a taco stand. We found Rosa in a narrow manual-crank hospital bed that occupied virtually the entire cubicle allotted to her. Her left leg was supported by Mexican-style traction: a bed sheet wrapped around the ankle and looped over the metal bar at the foot of the bed, where it was weighted by means of a plastic gallon water bottle partially filled with water. Although there was no room for even one chair, her bed was ringed with chattering family: sister, brother-in-law, niece, and two small grand-nephews. The bed itself was strewn with the fragrant remains of tacos and burritos and fresh chile sauce. Rosa looked small and pale but serene in the warm glow of family and food.

As a pediatrician, I had forgotten most of what little orthopedics I ever learned. But I remembered enough to know that time was of the essence in pinning a fractured hip, and I asked the nurse who came to greet us if we could speak to the orthopedic surgeon. "Ah, *señora*," the nurse told me, "regrettably the orthopedic surgeon is away in Guadalajara, but he should be back in a week or two." I must have blanched, because she hastened to add, "But if you wish, you can speak to the intern who is on duty here tomorrow. He, too, is an orthopedic doctor." I felt only marginally reassured, but the conversation was clearly over: the nurse was busy plumping up Rosa's pillow and smoothing back her hair.

Dr. Garcia, the intern, looked frighteningly young to me, but he exuded energy and confidence. Yes, he could certainly perform the required surgery—he knew the procedure well. All he needed were the necessary surgical instruments; he would order them from Mexico City immediately, and they should arrive within ten days. Ten days! Didn't this man realize that if Rosa were in a U.S. hospital she would already be on her first post-op day by now, up and moving? Gently, patiently, the young doctor pointed out that this was not a U.S. hospital, but was, rather, a small hospital in a small town in a poor country. High-tech surgical instruments were hard to come by. But perhaps—and his face lit up—perhaps the *señora* and her husband could purchase the instruments in California and bring them to Ensenada? He looked eager, a child peering through a shop window at a long-coveted toy.

After a wild drive north and hours of frantic searching, we finally located the appropriate surgical set in a medical supply store in San Diego. The salesman astounded me by offering to buy back any unused instruments after the surgery. Nothing in my medical training had prepared me for any part of this experience. Feeling like Alice in a weird wonderland, I paid the man, and we raced back south across the border with our sterile cargo. Dr. Garcia caressed the package with undisguised love: he could hardly wait to wrap his fingers around the smooth metal. *Mañana*, he promised. Tomorrow he would operate—provided, of course, that there was an operating room available, that there were enough nurses in the hospital, that our family had supplied enough blood. He disappeared with the surgical pack, smiling happily. I began to understand dimly that I was, indeed, moving through a world whose rules were utterly different than those of the crisp, efficient medical world I knew. Here was a world incomprehensibly poor in material resources, but vastly rich in humanity; and everything here depended on people: their ingenuity, their generosity, their love.

Of course there were plenty of willing blood donors among the family members. My husband and I phoned the hospital director at his home that evening to request his personal help in securing an operating room. We made the call from a small shop whose owner had opened after hours, especially for us, when Rosa's nurse sent us out to buy a surgical drain they would need. Finally, when Rosa was prepped and ready and lying on the gurney, my husband had to run to the corner store for nail polish remover to clean her manicured nails before she could go to the O.R. The nurse who wheeled her down the hall to surgery held her hand, murmuring endearments like a mother to a small child.

Rosa survived the surgery and eventually returned to her home outside Mexico City. But she never again walked without fear, and her spirit slowly withered away like a wild bird in captivity. She died almost two years later on Easter Sunday, *el domingo de la resurección*. Now whenever we visit the family in Mexico, we visit Rosa too, under the pepper tree where she lies with her parents and a brother who went before her. Children run and shout among the markers while just outside the gates of the *camposanto* the ice cream vendor plies his wares. And on some afternoons, when the air is warm with the scent of *masa* and chiles, a lone sparrow sings out from somewhere atop the pepper tree, its voice filling the air with a fine, sweet vibrato.

The Wreck

Una Nichols Hynum

No one saw what happened, no one ever witnesses
an accident, but we all heard the crash and grind of
metal, rushed out to see a pickup like a shiny black
beetle on its back waving monster tires in the air,
oozing golden fluids from the crushed body at
the intersection of Twenty-fourth and K. No one
was hurt. The driver squeezed out the window,
an ant crawling out a dead eye. Neighbors lined
the sidewalks, vines of children hung on fences.
The atmosphere turned festive. We cheered on the
Little Tramp driver from Tic-Tac-Towing as he flipped
her over, winched her onto the truck bed. The whole
body settled with a metallic sigh. A rainbow appeared
as if from a new box of crayons as he drove away,
the bent antenna waving and bowing to the crowd.

Changing a Light Bulb

Rick Seidenwurm

Changing a light bulb in the bedroom closet demands a wide variety of skills and close judgment calls. First, there's the issue of which ladder to use. The big seven-foot ladder is the popular choice, but the long winding trek from garage to bedroom typically results in both a pulled shoulder muscle and a major ding in the hallway stucco. The small stepladder is easier to transport and would most certainly be the right selection for ninety-nine percent of the adult population of the western world. But if you've been Guinness-certified as having the world's shortest arms, those same shoulder muscles will pay the price during small-ladder bulb-changing. Nevertheless, you usually choose the small ladder.

Place the small stepladder under the dusty fixture in the closet. Begin unscrewing the three screws that hold the dirty glass globe. Those screws are invariably too tight and at an awkward angle, making leverage almost impossible. This is the point when you curse the asshole who over-tightened those screws last time and then realize that the asshole was you.

Somehow the fixture finally comes loose, and you have to juggle it before gaining control. It is filled with dust balls and semi-decomposed insects, many of which resemble dust balls. Now descend the ladder with the fixture in tow, and proceed to the sink. Carefully clean the fixture with warm water and soap like your mother taught you, and then wash your hands, being sure to remove the dragonfly wings from under your fingernails. Dry fixture and set it aside.

Return to the closet and turn on the light switch. Observe which bulb is out. Turn off light switch and ascend ladder. Remove defective bulb without burning fingers and descend. Check wattage on bulb, and trek to garage cabinet to find correct replacement bulb. During return trip to bedroom, wonder why replacement bulbs for bedroom closet aren't kept in bedroom closet.

Ascend ladder with replacement bulb and screw in. Descend and turn on light switch to confirm that new bulb was not defective. Carefully ascend ladder holding bug-free fixture in your left hand. Use right hand to loosen the three screws a little more. If you need to switch hands, it is strongly recommended that you do so on the ground and not on the ladder.

Carefully place the domed fixture in its setting and begin screwing the screws in, alternating among them. You may want to switch hands at this point, but it is not recommended. This is where the shoulder starts to ache, but tough it out even when the angles seem impossible. And just when you think you have failed, the fixture will hold. It is recommended that you smile at this point, just before you realize you have once again overtightened the goddamn screws.

God, this was so much easier when there were two of us.

I Had Tea With Mary Oliver

Trish Dugger

I had tea with Mary Oliver
last evening. She droned
on and on about spring
violets in soft forest moss.
She lost me in a bog on
the edge of a pinewood.
I smiled and nodded in
response to her tedious
musings about peonies,
wildlife creatures, fawns
and bees, ants, while
I dreamed of dancing
in a peony pink gown,
sleek satin, a hand
sliding down my back,
like tea with honey
sliding down my throat.

The Woman Who Slept Upside Down

Sandra Block

Until her fortieth birthday Melinda was an ordinary woman: long-time wife, good mother to two not-so-small children. Her neighbors liked her and depended on her to get them through crises. She dressed in sensible blouses and pants that could be worn to the supermarket as well as to a middle school PTA meeting, where she described herself as "more of an Indian than a chief."

Her husband was a hard worker and a good eater, not very picky in his appetite so Melinda kept her cooking plain. She had only one cookbook, inherited from her late mother-in-law, which offered twenty-two ways to cook a chicken breast.

Melinda was quite diligent in her housework, so of course she could not work outside the home; the danger of dusty tabletops and waxy yellow build-up on the kitchen floor too much to risk. It was her particular routine to change all the bed linens once a week, necessary or not and she kept two sets of linen for each bed in rotation, one on the bed and one in the wash. There was a well-worn set of sheets on the sofa bed in the family room that she washed only twice a year. Her family never had any overnight guests so that schedule seemed sufficient to Melinda.

The family's routine in the evening was as well established as everything else in her tidy home. The children were in bed by nine o'clock, and Melinda and her husband would retire at ten o'clock after an hour of this television show or that, usually her husband's choice. This suited Melinda because, truth be told, she didn't really watch what was on the screen. Instead she would throw that switch she had, the one the husband had never known about (did anyone?), the switch that turned all her internal lights and schedules to low so Melinda could think nothing, feel nothing, and be nothing. She had discovered the switch early in her married life, one night when her husband was talking about his childhood and how happy he had been before all the responsibility of marriage and family arrived. It was his habit to lean over and kiss Melinda on the forehead at the end of his reminiscing and she found it imperative that she turn off sometime before the kiss. Earlier in the marriage she had wondered if this "turning off" was really normal and if other good wives and mothers had their own switch. But she was not the kind to pry so she never asked.

It was on a Thursday evening about two months earlier when the trouble started. With her husband already in bed (left side, no variations please) Melinda was about to get in on her side, placing her right hand as usual to smooth the already smooth pillowcase at the head of the bed. She was quite surprised to feel a vague dampness on the pillowslip, as if it had come out of the Kenmore dryer too soon and slipped over her foam pillow too soon. She stood by the bedside faintly bewildered with her hand still on the damp. She stood there for a few minutes before her husband noticed. He told her to come to bed. Truth be told, he first had the thought to ask her what was wrong but a funny flutter in his chest seemed to warn against the asking. But Melinda didn't come to bed. She looked at her husband, the man whose sleeping right side she had occupied for the past twelve years when she was struck, literally struck with the urge to sleep upside down. That is to say she desired more than anything to sleep with her head at the foot of the bed. She told him that the pillowslip was damp, and that the dampness had stained (that is the word she used—stained—which he thought very odd) the top sheet. Instead of remaking the bed, which he must agree would disturb him no end, she thought she would sleep tonight, just this one night with her head at the other end, at the foot of the bed.

Her husband thought this was exceedingly odd, but he thought that disturbing his rest was even more intolerable so with a scowl meant to convey disapproval, he told Melinda to suit herself. She pulled up the sheets tucked tightly at the bed foot and crawled in and her husband turned out his bedside lamp. That was the first night.

But not the last night. Melinda found that life had changed in two very strange and wonderful ways from that night on. The pillowslip and top sheet at the head of the bed on her side (no variations!) remained damp. The first morning she had washed and dried the second set of sheets for her bed, drying the linens for an extra ten minutes just to be sure, and made up the bed. That night, and every night, she found the same damp touch on her clean linens, only at the topside of the bed, only on her side.

The second most wonderful change involved her dreaming. Melinda had never remembered her dreams before. In fact she believed that she did not dream, although Dr. Levy, the psychologist whose lecture she had attended at the PTA meeting, the psychologist who came to talk about sleep disorders in children, the man who she approached afterward with a plate of homemade cookies as her excuse, assured her that everyone dreams. She remembered she did not like his suggestion that there might be somewhere in her mind where her dreams were kept and waiting to be heard, as if there were something wrong with Melinda's mind.

But now, at the foot of the bed, Melinda remembered her dreams, all of them, every morning. They were most wonderful, filled with strange and interesting people Melinda had never met, people dressed in colors of sunlight, moonlight and flowers. Melinda joined the people in her dreams, dressed in her own colors of rainstorms, dawns and seashells; she joined them in travels to places of music and dancing. Melinda remembered all of her dreams at the foot of her bed.

Her husband and children were very confused at first, when Melinda continued to sleep upside down. At the beginning it was odd when at night her husband would think of something he wanted Melinda to do or cook or fetch in the morning. He would turn to tell her and find himself addressing ten toes resting on the pillow top. There was no point in that so he stopped giving Melinda instructions at night and took to keeping a small notebook at his bedside table where he would remind himself to do this or that in the morning. Instead, he began talking to Melinda's ten toes about what had gone right or wrong in his days and about the small shaker of baby powder he kept in his office desk, about how the scent of it reminded him of the sweetness of their children's small baby heads, about how the scented memory soothed him.

It was the same with her two children. At first, they screamed every morning at her feet to get up and carry their worries and fears for them, to help them rush through their days so as to get to grown-uphood as soon as possible. But Melinda's feet would not act on their demands; they would only listen and wait for the children to be children. And so her children stopped screaming and began whispering to their mother's toes about their own daydreams and nightmares.

About one month into remembering her dreams, Melinda began to act strangely during her days as well. She no longer dressed in sensible blouses and pants, instead she wore long gauzy skirts embroidered with tiny mirrors and tinier bells that tinkled when she walked. She wrapped long silvery shawls around her brilliant silk shirts, colored of glossy gardenia leaves, so to give an effect of shafts of moonlight swirling around a dreamy garden. This disturbed the sensibly dressed mothers at the PTA meetings. Melinda appeared not to notice—or perhaps she did but did not care.

In the second month of remembering her dreams, Melinda was still sleeping upside down in her bed when she wrote a letter to her husband, leaving it on his pillow one morning. He found it that evening after Melinda had already retired. He didn't like to wake her with his bedside lamp, so he slipped out to the kitchen where he stood by the nightlight always lit over the breakfast table.

My dear husband,

In this life there are miracles everyday. I have found that miracles do not arrive in thunderclaps or great pillars of smoke; instead, miracles appear in silly, ordinary packages delivered everyday to our doorstep. Things like lizards warming themselves on garden walls or a sunrise that appears every morning. Miracles of memories of warm, powdery infant heads filled with future loves and hopes. Now I understand the miracle of a pillowslip that refuses to stay dry, I understand that a lifetime of tears cried at the head of a bed will never dry, and that a lifetime of dreams, dreams that have not gone away, only slipped to the bed foot, will be waiting for me. I have seen your dreams, dear, piled up years deep at the foot of the bed, across from where I lay my head every night. Waiting.

    Melinda's husband stood at the nightlight with her note in his hand and considered. After long minutes he walked down the hall and into their bedroom finally sitting on his side of the bed and looking, first at Melinda's toes resting on the pillow top and then at her face, dreaming at the bed foot. He still held her note in his right hand and, for a moment, he stretched his left hand to feel his pillowcase, stopping just short of touch. Instead, he turned to open the drawer of his bedside table and slid her note inside, closing the drawer softly. Then he turned to the bed foot, gently pulled up the loosely-tucked sheets and slipped in next to his wife.

ALL I WANT IS TO STOP WANTING

Lizz Huerta

all I want is to stop wanting

evolution, I am above these buses you throw
      me under. I ask, reptile brain, that you end these

irrational impulses to chase worthless options;
      namely stud, loner, the tasty aloof and emotional

inhabitants of never-never land I can't
      seem to stop digging my teeth into. despite

what my hips broadcast I am not the kind
      of woman who wants to be filled with kicking

feet or ever have to deal with teething or any
      other bones fighting their way out of flesh.

enough then with the hunters grunting around,
      enough with my dumb tongue hanging, I'm no

beast in heat scaling high fences, let me live loosed—
      let me begin believing in safer things than you.

Midwest

Jess Jollett

We placed ourselves in the middle lands. Journeyed far from coastlines and debt collectors. We had thought about giving ourselves new names, but decided that was just cliché. Eddie told me I didn't have to work. "Won't that be nice, baby? You can just be my little housewife." I tried to cook things to make Eddie forget we were in a snow blizzard, like *mole* and *papusas* and *chorizo*. But nothing was ever hot enough. It was like this place was impervious to our energy. I could not dance anymore, I could not sing. I was even forgetting our language.

Contributors

Deborah Harding-Allbritain's poems have appeared in numerous publications and anthologies, including: *The Antioch Review; The Taos Review; In the Palm of Your Hand; The Poet's Portable Workshop; The Unmade Made Bed: Sensual Writing on Married Love; Stand Up Poetry: The Anthology; Autism Digest; Perigee Publication for the Arts; Genre; Michigan Quarterly Review; Whole Wide World: Poets and Poems Anthology;* and *My Writers Circle: List of Interesting Poets.* A native Californian, Deborah works as a speech pathologist in San Diego.

Tria Andrews has published critical essays, fiction, poetry, and photography. She is a graduate of the MFA program in Fiction at San Diego State University and currently resides in San Diego, where she mentors for the American Indian Recruitment program and teaches yoga to incarcerated adolescents.

Scott Barbour is a member of San Diego Writers, Ink, and a regular at Thursday Writers. His work was featured on *First Friday CD of Year 3.* He says he's working on a novel, but he really just likes to look cool posing as a writer at local coffee shops.

Born in Baltimore, Maryland, **Sandra Block** lives in San Diego with her husband Jeff and son Asher. She is a clinical psychologist in private practice, adjunct faculty at Argosy University, and a writer at heart. "The Woman Who Slept Upside Down" is her first published fiction.

Judy Goldstein Botello has practiced pediatrics in San Diego since 1973, and has taught and lectured widely. Currently, she works as a physician consultant to the San Diego Regional Center. Dr. Goldstein Botello is the author of three nonfiction books and of numerous articles, book reviews, and poems.

Jackie Bouchard's day job involves writing boring reports about the scientific research database publishing market. (Yaaaaawn.) In her spare time, Jackie writes humorous fiction. After living in Bermuda, Canada, and on both US coasts, Jackie, her husband, and their beagle chose San Diego. *What the Dog Ate* is her first novel.

Celeste Carpenter lives in Southern California with her husband, where she works as a technical writer, but tries really hard to be creative in her off-hours. Not counting the poems published in her school's fifth grade literary journal, this is her first publication.

William Cass is a school administrator in San Diego. He has published a number of short stories in smaller literary magazines such as *The Insider*, *Red Wheelbarrow*, *Bellowing Ark*, and *ESC-Magazine*.

Charlie Daly is a transplant from Boston. He lives in Ocean Beach and attends the University of San Diego. His passions include surfing, words, spicy tuna rolls, and Newbreak Coffee. He reads Carver, Hemingway, Hunter Thompson, Burroughs, and all the other great alcoholics.

Trish Dugger, Poet Laureate of Encinitas, featured at 2009 Border Voices Poetry Fair, has been published in *Magee Park Poets* and other San Diego area anthologies, and in *California Quarterly* and *Spillway*. Her poem "Spare Parts" was published on Ted Kooser's americanlifeinpoetry.org.

Alysia Everett is a writer and a student at Mira Costa College who resides in Oceanside, California. She is currently working on a memoir based on the events of her father's death and the aftermath.

Crystal Hadidian grew up in Austin, Texas; graduated from the University of California, Santa Barbara and is now studying at SDSU. It is worth noting that the childbirth labor depicted in her poem is much more miserable sounding than her actual experience, which was a peaceful water birth with no screaming of any sort.

Randy Herman is Ryan, Tad, and Chapin's dad. He's also a recovering actor and hangs out in Bankers Hill and Del Mar with Jill, Sappho, and Mambo. Between offbeat writing challenges and pick-up football games he practices Marriage and Family Therapy and writes plays for the stage.

Poet **Lizz Huerta** lives and writes in South Park. She spends many hours watching the man who lives down the alley from her weld odd, metal objects to his roof at all hours of the night. She feels blessed to live in such a creative and fertile community.

Una Nichols Hynum, a finalist for the James Hearst Poetry Prize, most recently published in *A Year in Ink*, vols. 1 and 2; *Magee Park Anthology*; *Oasis Journal*; *San Diego Poetry Annual*; *The Writer's Digest*; and *Margie*.

Marianne S. Johnson holds a BA from Cal Poly, San Luis Obispo, and a law degree from the UC, Hastings College of the Law. She is married with two children, and a practicing attorney in San Diego. Her poetry is published in *Lavanderia: A Mixed Load of Women, Wash and Word*, and is forthcoming in *Calyx* and *Sport Literate* in 2010.

After running away to the Midwest, **Jess Jollett**, a homegrown townie, returned to San Diego to work out her savior's complex through employment at the American Civil Liberties Union. Often, when she gets home, she writes short-shorts about her angst-filled twenties and the women in her family.

Clifton King is a Southern California poet, a grandfather, and pursuer of the perfect wave. His poetry has appeared in various publications.

Although many people think that poets don't earn much money, **Steve Kowit** and the best-selling romance novelist Nora Roberts have a combined annual income of $60 million! His most recent book is *Crossing Borders*, a collaboration with the artist Lenny Silverberg (Spuyten Duyvil Press).

Eber Lambert has been an engineering manager and mercurial writer of short fiction and poetry in San Diego for twenty-six years. He hosts the New Poetic Brew Open Mic in South Park, chisels away at his Sisyphean novel project, and still buys vinyl records and CDs.

Sylvia Levinson's publishing credits include *Snowy Egret*; *Blue Arc West*; *City Works*; *Hunger and Thirst*; *A Year in Ink*, vols. 1 and 2; *Magee Park*; *Poetic Matrix*; and *Christian Science Monitor*. Awards include City Works, 2007; American Society on Aging; and San Diego African-American Writers and Artists. Her book, *Gateways: Poems of Nature, Meditation and Renewal* is available at www.sylvialevinson.com.

Fred Longworth restores vintage audio components for a living. He was ousted from Coffeehouses Anonymous for sneaking caffeine tablets into his Perrier. He sees Joseph Stalin in the eyes of most reformers. He has been published in *California Quarterly*, *Pearl*, *Rattapallax*, *Spillway*, and many others—but who really cares?

A freelance advertising copywriter in San Diego, **Tori Malcangio** crafts real estate zingers, amusement park radio, and with whatever time is leftover, writes fiction and nonfiction. Publications include: *ZYZZYVA*, *SmokeLong Quarterly*, *The San Diego Reader*, *VerbSap*, *Pearl Magazine*, *Literary Mama*, and a notable story finalist in the 2009 Open City RRofihe trophy prize. An unnamed short story collection is in the works.

Seretta Martin is the author of *Foreign Dust Familiar Rain* and is an *Atlanta Review* finalist. Her review of Anna Swir is forthcoming on Web Del Sol. Seretta nurtures creativity in youth by teaching Border Voices and California Poets in the Schools poetry. She hosts Barnes & Noble Poetry Series, La Mesa. Her award-winning poems are well published in the US and abroad.

When not writing bios or sonnets in bathroom stalls, **David Tomas Martinez** lurks along the trolley lines giving hugs to the girls and pounds to the homeboys, all the while remarking how the cigarette butts on the ground look like petals on a wet, black bough.

Patrick McMahon is a San Diego writer, photographer, and musician. His completed, unpublished memoir, *Becoming Patrick*, is a sensitive exploration of identity by means of re-connecting with blood relatives after growing up adopted. He can be contacted at pj@patrickmc.com.

John Mullen lives in Poway with his wife, Susan. He is currently writing a mystery in which Dick, a Digitally Integrated Consciousness, seeks out his creator's killer. "The Dance Card" is John's first published work. He thanks his fellow writers who commented on an earlier draft.

Oriana (Ivy Warwick) was born in Poland. She came to the United States when she was seventeen. Her publications include *Poetry, Ploughshares, Best American Poetry 1992, Nimrod, New Letters, The Iowa Review, American Poetry Review, Prairie Schooner,* and *Southern Poetry Review*. She has worked as a journalist and college instructor. She lives in Chula Vista.

Bill Peters grew up in northern Minnesota and moved to California twenty years ago. Over the years, memories of his family and childhood have been brought to life by years of practice with Thursday Writers and DimeStories. He is currently teaching and tutoring mathematics at San Diego Mesa College.

Cat Saint Martin's poetry has been published in *The Muse Strikes Back: A Poetic Response by Women to Men*, *The Temple*, *The Long Island Quarterly*, and *5x7: A New York Anthology*. She was a Bread Loaf Writers' Conference participant and grant recipient of the Italian-American Foundation. Previously an editor for *Vox Populi Anthology of the Seattle Poetry Festival*, Cat has read her poetry mainly in US coastal cities. She currently lives in San Diego with her husband and two sons.

Rick Seidenwurm is a mostly-retired corporate attorney with a surprisingly fertile imagination. He much prefers writing short stories to nasty lawyer letters. Rick has served for several years as a director and the treasurer of San Diego Writers, Ink. He is fortunate to have learned the writing craft from Judy Reeves.

Since relocating to San Diego in 1998 from the Northeast, **Gerald Vanderpot** has lived in Hillcrest. Besides working and writing, he is active in his union. Gerald has published in *San Diego City Works* and *Boston Literary Magazine*. "47 Book Titles from My-Shelf" is a dedication to his influences.

Jeanine Webb's work has appeared in *ZYZZYVA*, *Louis Liard Magazine*, and *Spectrum*. She earned her MA in Creative Writing at University of California, Davis, where she taught poetry. Her manuscript, *Flash Paper*, was a finalist for the Cider Press Review Book Award. She lives in San Diego and grew up in Encinitas.

Lauren Wilensky graduated with a BA from SDSU. Currently, she is an advisor and teacher at San Diego Met High School. During the summer she teaches at the San Diego Area Writing Project's Young Writers' Camp. She lives with her husband, cat, and two dogs.

Jennifer Brooke Williamson is a San Diego native who'd let you win the Scrabble game just to see you smile. She is currently earning an MFA in Fiction from SDSU, and holds a BA in Creative Writing from San Francisco State University.

Amy Wolf is a second-year graduate student at the School of International Relations and Pacific Studies at the University of California, San Diego. Before moving to San Diego, she taught English in South Korea for fourteen months.

Al Zolynas's books include *The New Physics* (Wesleyan University Press, 1979); *Under Ideal Conditions*, winner of the San Diego Book Award for Best Poetry, 1994 (Laterthanever Press); and *The Same Air* (Intercultural Studies Forum, 1997). A long-time Zen practitioner, he teaches at Alliant International University in San Diego.

EDITORS

Roger Aplon was a founder and Managing Editor of CHOICE Magazine with John Logan and Aaron Siskind. He has published eight collections of poetry, the most recent being *The Man With His Back To The Room*, and one of prose, *Intimacies*. After seven years living and writing in Barcelona, Spain, he returned to San Diego in 2007 where he now teaches writing workshops independently and with San Diego Writers, Ink. He occasionally reads his work with musicians from the experimental music groups Wormhole and  The Trummerflora Collective. He has recently been awarded an arts fellowship from the Helene Wurlitzer Foundation (Summer 2009) in Taos, New Mexico. You can see and hear examples of his work at: www.rogeraplon.com

Jennifer Silva Redmond is Editor-in-Chief of Sunbelt Publications, an award-winning small press. Her stories have appeared in *Science of Mind*, *Cruising World*, and *Latinos in Lotusland: An Anthology of Contemporary Southern California Literature*. Co-founder of the critically acclaimed *Sea of Cortez Review* (1998-2001), she enjoys speaking to groups of readers and writers, and is on the staff of the Southern California Writers Conference. She and artist-writer-teacher Russel Redmond live on their sailboat, where they are at work on their third screenplay.

San Diego Writers, Ink is a nonprofit literary organization that nurtures writers and those wishing to explore the craft of writing, fosters a literary community, promotes literature, and celebrates artistic diversity.

The Ink Spot, located in the Art Center Lofts in San Diego's East Village, is our gathering place where we offer classes, groups, workshops, readings, and other literary events. The Ink Spot is also home to the Arts Council Gallery, which features the work of local artists.

SDW, Ink collaborates with other artistic, cultural, and community organizations throughout the city and county to promote literature and to inspire the community of writers.

We are grateful to The Merci Fund at the San Diego Foundation for its generous support, and to Steve Gould for his generosity.

San Diego Writers, Ink
P.O. Box 34374
San Diego, CA 92163

The Ink Spot
710 13th St., Studio 210
San Diego, CA 92101

www.sandiegowriters.org

Order additional copies of *A Year in Ink, Volume 1* (2008), edited by Thomas Larson; *Volume 2* (2009), edited by Sandra Alcosser and Arthur Salm; and *Volume 3* (2010), edited by Roger Aplon and Jennifer Silva Redmond, at our website.

LaVergne, TN USA
20 January 2010
170597LV00001B/1/P